Charlie's Bubble

Beka Flynn

Published by Brickhaven Books, 2024.

This is a work of fiction. Similarities to real people, places, or events are entirely coincidental.

CHARLIE'S BUBBLE

First edition. August 1, 2024.

Copyright © 2024 Beka Flynn.

ISBN: 979-8227895837

Written by Beka Flynn.

Table of Contents

Dedicated to my love, the real Charlie.

Time is not a rigid straight line, but a soft shadow floating on the never-ending ocean. It's constantly drifting in and out of the super wormholes. Filling these ceaseless entities of time and space are hundreds of virtual bubbles. They are secretly connected, merging and overlapping, growing and diminishing.

Prologue

October 2020. San Diego.

Overlooking the rolling valleys of Southern California, the Palomar Valley Hospital stood tall and towering over the dusky green carpet and brown peaks laid down by nature. As the golden hue touched these creations, tranquility settled in and the sunlight glistening on the turquoise glass adorning the hospital building, made it seem like a large shining shield protecting its patients from all the miseries.

Watching, absorbing, and basking in such beauty, with his face pressed against the wide glass window, was Charlie.

Settled on the sixth floor of the hospital, he glanced out at the play of light and shadow falling over the folds of the overlooking valley. Those same beautiful, deep, brown-green eyes looked out in childlike joy. Though the slight vicissitudes of life had altered it a bit, his face was still chiseled and handsome with a high nose and full lips. His body had slightly thickened but still stood tall and straight while his hair showed hints of grey.

No one could guess that he was seventy years old.

Even she said the same. She always said that she saw the seven-year-old boy from the old photo on his clearly mature face: slightly raised, with distinctive, handsome features, a bright smile without any shadow, and happiness rippling in his eyes.

He had gone from seven to seventy and yet, nothing had changed. He was exactly the same as he had been.

It was as if his aging skin was merely a meaningless disguise for a still innocent soul.

The light of happiness poured out from his eyes, bright, dazzling, transparent, and crystal clear, without a trace of impurity or haze.

That was what she saw when he smiled; expecting her to nestle into his arms.

She saw his joy in her, and his dependence on her; his dependence on her for his entire life, for everything he had.

And her heart melted.

The medical equipment and oximeter, just a few moments before hitched to Charlie's body, now laid scattered on the bed. He had them removed before going to the bathroom. But today, instead of taking his usual route from the bathroom to the bed, he slowly staggered his weak body to the window and looked out.

As he lost himself in the ethereal beauty outside the window, his mind drifted towards her, and he fumbled for his phone in his pocket. That same ingenuous, childlike joy again flickered in his sparkling eyes as he dialed her number.

"I finally got a chance to look outside. The windows are so big. You can't imagine how beautiful the outside view is! I can see the valley stretching far away, the blue of the mountains, and the plains... so green."

His smile played between his awe towards the beauty in front of him and his rich beaming joy at the response of his company. For the brief moment, he almost forgot how sick he was. The temporarily revived life disguised the short breath in his voice.

"By the way, I recognized 78 and finally figured out the location. That night the ambulance went round and round for a long time, so I thought I was being taken to a hospital far, far away. 78 is usually packed with heavy traffic, but it's almost empty now. It's like a ghost town. Incredible!

Yes, it is very nice. The hospital is new and modern; almost like a hotel. If it wasn't for being sick, I would have loved to stay here with such a beautiful view and see the world with you.

Sure, I'll take some pictures for you shortly."

Charlie heard someone calling him from behind. He glanced back and whispered to the phone that the nurse needed to take his temperature.

"I'll talk to you later. Love you."

Charlie quietly hung up the phone and moved back to the hospital bed, one step following another, pausing in between to catch his breath.

The nurse checked his temperature, blood pressure and heartbeat, all the measurements on the vitals chart, every hour. "The doctor ordered a few more tests to see what's going on." The nurse informed before she left.

Charlie kept lying on the bed.

A few minutes of standing seemed to have exhausted the energy left in his body. At this moment, he could only lie there, motionless, like a withered plant, with no breath of life at all, silently spread out on the bed.

Fallen like a collapsed ruin.

Like the end of life. Or more precisely, the end of *this* life, in *this* dimension.

The life that he had chosen but not been born into.

The life that had started with the Bubble in the Caribbean back in 1978.

The life with *her*.

He could only plead with his withering body, begging it to cheer up and allow him to go on a little further.

To allow him to see her, *just one more time.*

Charlie felt a familiar wave of heat inside his left ear, followed by brief sensation of tickling, as if an extremely tiny lady bug was crawling through.

He smiled faintly, now alone in the empty room.

It was Bill initiating a call from the other end of their private line via a biofilm implanted in his ear, from *the past*.

The past was still there, in the present to him, waiting for him. The past that he had abandoned.

"Charlie!" Bill shouted.

"Bill?" Charlie responded in a weak voice.

"Listen, you must come back right away." Bill sounded anxious.

"You can't delay any longer! Millions of people are dying! *You are dying*!!

I can't just watch you die. Charlie, *please, leave the Bubble.*" Bill was pleading.

Charlie remained silent for a long while, breathing a bit unevenly.

"No." He finally whispered, firmly.

Part One Freedom
A1

SUMMER, 1976. LOUISIANA.

The faint morning fog was gradually dissipating to the touch of the nascent sunlight. Still drowned in sleep, the sprawling Hammond Northshore regional airport stood lonely and deserted, waiting for the world to come alive.

Only a white Aerostar, a small plane with twin engines, slipped quietly out of the hangar. The word "Paradise" was printed on the fuselage.

Charlie was sitting, all geared, in the cockpit. Twenty-six years old, Charlie had the perfect Marlon Brando's sexy face, complimented by his lean figure.

Three beautiful girls took their seats behind him, chattering, excited and curious. One of them was Jennifer, his girlfriend.

The plane taxied gracefully onto the long runway of 6,500 feet.

A runway that Charlie knew all too well.

Accelerate.

Take off.

This was a high-end private mini aircraft with mid-length wings and cantilevers, with an ability to cover up to 1178 kilometers in one leg.

Charlie had bought it as a gift to himself on his birthday about two years ago, and had flown it frequently since. He had eventually become bored with all the common destinations within the States.

His destination this time was a bit out of the regular map and legally prohibited-the coast near Havana, Cuba—the unfamiliar communist country, rich in cigars. From there, they were bound to board a boat to Nassau Island in the Bahamas off Bermuda.

He had long wanted to go there to check things out even just superficially. He always had the curiosity for something forbidden to him. He refused to automatically accept any boundary set by people. Rules were made to break and deeper truth drowned by the noise of public opinions would be revealed. So as he started to entertain the idea of expanding his air travel, Charlie deliberately chose Cuba instead of Miami to get to Nassau in the Caribbean, for fun.

Now through the plane window, the airport slowly shrank, and soon the outline of New Orleans appeared, followed by the gleaming gray–blue waters of the Gulf of Mexico.

Young Charlie soared like a giant bird, sitting at the helm. The early morning sun bloomed and dyed the sky orange and pink. The front propeller kept spinning.

The sea sloped, then flattened, filling up the view.

The ever-expanding landscape appeared to be resting on a colossal slab trying to maintain its balance. It swayed and leaned to the side outside the window of Charlie's plane.

Charlie maintained the altitude within 25 feet of the gulf. The plane soared low above the sea like an emerging white seagull.

This way, he was able to evade radar surveillance. To this end, Charlie had also sprayed a special coating on the fuselage to absorb any potential radar waves. It was important for him to approach Cuba without being seen.

He and the girls had only their passports with them; no special licenses, or visa permission to enter Cuba.

Nearly two hours into the flight over the calm ocean brought the Cuba Island into view.

Charlie maneuvered to descend near Playa Baracoa airport outside Havana—a very humble airport with no monitoring station; an open flat, and a simple blue bungalow. The airport building stood plain and rough, like an elongated matchbox that could be easily crushed.

As they landed, the plane taxied slowly, and finally stopped in a carefully chosen remote corner.

Charlie killed the engine and turning around, patted Jennifer on her curvy ass as she stood up. Her exaggerated scream was followed by the girls while Charlie got off the plane.

Once on the ground, they all immediately became quiet. Hiding their nervousness, they walked cautiously toward the blue house.

As they entered, they found the house quite empty, save for a row of plastic chairs against the wall, with pictures of airplanes pasted onto the walls.

Two short, dark-skinned women in white shirts, dark blue dresses, and black stockings sat inside. They were Cuban flight attendants. They were speaking Spanish and appeared to be just off work.

Nobody was paying any attention to Charlie and the girls. Everything went just as they had wished.

They passed through the hall without being stopped and were soon standing in an open field.

The concrete floor was jagged, cracked, and filled with green moss. Lack of maintenance was visibly evident. Not far away stood some lush trees, adding to the authority of nature over the place.

Charlie stopped and stared into the distance.

He knew that a beach was nearby.

A figure emerged from the woods and started walking towards them.

"Charlie, are we in trouble?" Jennifer asked nervously.

"Of course not." Charlie's mouth curled into a smile.

The figure approached quickly: a Cuban man, tanned, thin, and wrinkled; half a cigar hanging from the corner of his mouth.

He went straight to Charlie with a big smile on his face.

"Welcome to Cuba!" He removed his cigar and hugged Charlie warmly.

A2

In the early years, Riel had fled by boat from Cuba to Miami and opened a cigar shop there. It was there that he had met Charlie. Recently he had to go back to Cuba to take care of his aging mother who loved Fidel Castro. According to Charlie's arrangement, Riel was the one who would be getting them a boat.

As the greetings died down, Riel led everyone through several bright-colored, dilapidated but hustling streets, to the corner of the coast.

A boat appeared to be moored there quietly, disguised under an old and dusty black plastic cover that had collected lots of fallen leaves.

Riel stepped forward and lifted the plastic sheet, revealing a half-new light-blue convertible yacht.

Riel turned to Charlie.

"That's all I can do. I know you wanted something fancier, but that would attract too much attention. A Cuban doctor earns only $25 a month. It's a real Miami yacht, much better than a Cuban refugee boat."

Charlie jumped into the boat and set about examining it, striding back and forth.

"Um. Not bad. Thanks, Riel." Charlie handed over an envelope of cash to Riel.

Guided by Riel, Charlie and the girls spent the rest of the day roaming the colorful and dilapidated streets of Playa Baracoa. On the narrow and potholed streets were mostly wooden sheds with shutters. Castro's face was sometimes seen painted on the wall, reminding them that they were illegally in his territory. They could not help but feel jittery whenever someone was coming close to them. It wouldn't be fun to be arrested in Cuba! It was sure enough a quick glimpse of the country for Charlie. Soon later that day, they anxiously hopped on the yacht, destined towards the marvelous Nassau, Bahamas.

It was a sunny day and the balmy breeze flowing in from the sea made it so much more refreshing. It blew off all their nervousness about Cuba and promised a truly fun-filled adventure ahead! Charlie avoided the crowded port and docked near the quiet and secluded Love Beach of Nassau Island. The white sandy beach slowly sank into the crystal-clear waters. The Atlantic Ocean spreading its intoxicating blue under the bubbly white clouds looked as if imprinted on a postcard. It was like a secret paradise hidden behind the buildings and trees.

For a brief moment Charlie was overwhelmed by the serene beauty of the Caribbean island. He stood at the edge of the beach, gazing at the colossal ocean; the water brushing against his feet. He squatted down and scooped up a handful of white sand. He examined the wet chunks of fine sand crystals in his palm with curiosity. *Was it different from what he had seen?*

Breaking from his trance, Charlie noticed that the girls had already taken off their clothes and donned their bikinis. They all cheerfully gathered around him and posed for a group picture. Before Charlie could even react to it, they started to run towards the ocean in excitement.

Charlie soon followed, quickly throwing off his clothes, leaving only the gray-blue swimming trunks on. He followed Jennifer straight into the ocean and jumped into the water with a huge splash.

Jennifer seemed to be right in front of him, like a bright red buoy floating up and down in the gentle waves.

Charlie pushed forward with powerful strokes.

He cut through the tide and was soon deep into the ocean, far from the shore.

The bright blue sky seemed to have melted. It sank softly, layer by layer, disintegrating into countless light-weighted, crystal-like sunlight spots. The suspended crystal grains filled up the air- floating, flickering, dancing, and eventually settling on the surface of the boundless ocean, dazzling and blinding; distracting Charlie.

In the spur of the moment, he took a deep breath and dived straight into the ocean.

The sunlight being shielded by the water, everything instantaneously began thinning out, losing its hustle and bustle. The loud rumble of the ocean breeze as well as the waves suddenly became distant. Charlie was suddenly surrounded by nothing but peaceful quietness.

As he slowly floated down into the bottomless ocean, his body also became light, as fluid as water. It became a seaweed that swayed slowly with the waves.

He seemed to have completely forgotten about Jennifer, indulging in this isolated, almost weightless joy.

A lonely joy of freedom, escape, or exile.

He started diving deeper.

Above his head, the large rays of sunlight rippled on the water. The outlines of coral reefs under the sea were now vaguely visible to Charlie. A little phosphorescent silverfish swam by breaking Charlie's solitude.

A sense of joy flashed in him.

But it was immediately doused by what he saw next! A red snapper!

It first appeared on his left, just some bright red color in his field of vision. It appeared like the red silk that Chinese people wear for their celebrations, fluttering in the dim water.

He didn't pay much attention at first, he was busy calculating his time in the water.

Three minutes. Not wearing any diving gear, he'd been trying to make it to the three minutes underwater.

Beyond three minutes, it would be *death*.

Suddenly, a white beam of intense light focused into the water, striking the red snapper that was now placed quite close to himself. It had already swum up to him during his lack of attention, and the white light drenched it, illuminating its scales mixed with red and silver.

The round eyes of the red snapper moved and met his eyes. *Those eyes! That contact!* Those eyes did not feel as if they belonged to just a fish. They seemed to be possessed by a human soul, searching for human contact, exchanging meaningful glances with him.

A rush of cold shivers went down his spine. He suddenly felt an inexplicable fear groping on his heart; the isolated peace was long lost now.

The seemingly simple and innocent red snapper had now transformed into a suspicious creature as if it was, in fact, the disguise of a strange but powerful intellectual creature.

That chill again pressed against his back and clutched onto him.

Now, something even weirder happened.

The water slowly transformed into something more viscous, stagnant, and was no longer flowing freely. It was like a vacuole filled with transparent glue.

The glue seemed to trap the red snapper like ensnaring a tiny flying insect. The fish stopped swinging, and its body began to collapse, as if being crushed, stretched, and softened by an invisible force, and turned into a flat and thin red projection.

Then the projection slowly broke down, as if it was being digested until it disappeared completely.

Charlie was horrified to witness all this, and a sudden panic arose within him.

Nothing could explain what had just happened!

The mysterious and invisible force—the force that changed the water, the force that devoured the red snapper; *he was no rival for it at all.*

He instinctively turned around, wanting to escape.

As his mind dwelt in these thoughts, he felt something strange on his skin—tickling, warm, like a woman's eager kiss.

He tried to move his limbs, only to find that his body had become powerless. Suddenly pressure began to compress him into a thin membrane. No pain touched him, but the sense of disintegration was imprinted on his mind. As if someone had sucked his breath from him, he felt himself crushed into a thin film. As he floated in the water, he was further losing mass and dissipating in the sea, although his consciousness remained intact and awake.

His consciousness and body were being separated bizarrely. He felt as if he could look down at his body, which was turning soft and transparent.

But the fear in his mind slowly dissipated now. Strangely, he was instead getting immersed in an almost pleasant curiosity and confusion.

He felt safe and free. He felt protected, as if his soul, or the being that was capable of perception, emotion, and consciousness, was guarded in a safe bubble. And he was simply watching a fun thriller movie playing out on the watery screen in front of him.

A three-dimensional movie in which his body was directly participating.

His curiosity was tremendously aroused.

He felt like he was starting to shrink.

The translucent sphere of swelling sunlight rose higher and higher over the sea as if the blue dome was rising rapidly and receding above and beyond its space. Coral reefs on the ocean floor vanished beneath. Dense, dim waters shrouded his field of vision, and a turbulence of light and shadow began playing around him.

He continued to shrink until he became as tiny as a droplet of water, a minute unit of light and shadow himself.

He felt he was about to cease to exist. He felt his disappearance now inevitably hanging in front of him.

At this instant, a huge transparent bubble unexpectedly appeared right in front of his eyes.

It was crystal clear but with millions of colors fleeting and radiating on its surface.

He leaned in, pulled by the magnitudes of the reflections, and looked closely. He was left in sheer shock by his discovery.

A3

Pictures and colors floated within the surface of the bubble, like random movies overlapping and running at high speed.

A man in medieval European attire, driving a carriage down a path among the trees.

A towering ancient church filled with the humming of prayers and worship songs, sung by the chorus standing next to burning candles.

A lonely old man sitting alone, lost in his thoughts, in a deep alley.

A wild duck, startled by a sound at dusk, fluttering its wings and flying out of a cool lake into the thick of twilight.

The silent scenes were constantly switched and played out as if a child was playing with the remote control, switching between different channels, telling innumerable stories.

Endless fragmented episodes of the stories moved and bounced in front of Charlie.

Charlie's fascination with the bubble overpowered his every thought. That he was alone in the vast Atlantic was almost forgotten at this moment.

All he knew was his body, disappearing amidst all the deep sounds of the ocean and the high-pitched whistles of dolphins in the distance.

Suddenly he noticed something familiar; the silhouette of the red snapper that had just disappeared, once again floated in front of him. It was intact, swimming happily, combing through the seaweed.

But it didn't notice him this time. It swam away, waving its tail haphazardly.

The red snapper was not dead. It had simply existed in a different place.

He almost cried out with joy.

The bubble suddenly pushed close to him, floating on an unexpected wave. He felt the bubble touching his face. His soft shadow-like body was soaked in by the bubble, fusing, immersing him completely into its pictures.

Until it devoured him.

Strange noises surrounded him as his eyes slowly flickered to life. As he regained his consciousness, he felt his head bursting with a weird heaviness. Slowly sitting up, he found himself stranded on a strange street. *People were everywhere!* Under the lush locust trees along the street, at various shops, some going about their way, some shouting; people were everywhere—*Chinese people.*

While he took in the sudden change in his surroundings, he noticed a group of young people with white ribbons on their heads marching on the street, holding banners, and shouting slogans passionately.

He stood up and walked towards them. But he soon found himself surrounded by a growing crowd of engaged spectators. He could not understand a word the people were saying but they were surely agitated.

He tried to figure out the situation he was in. His headache made it worse and did nothing to clear his confusion.

The march had just passed when a police car showed up right behind with its sirens blaring hard.

Suddenly, somewhere from the crowd, a fire on a wooden stick flew out and landed on the police car, which had now been forced to slow down.

The police car stopped immediately and officers in government liveries rushed out of the attacked vehicle. Its siren kept spinning, like an enraged rooster cocking its feathers, filling the air with anger and agitation.

The crowd, which had by now an ominous sense about what was about to happen, became chaotic and started to scatter like panicking ants.

Charlie instinctively walked away, attempting to get out of all this turmoil.

How did I come here? Where are the girls?

Escaping from the panicking crowd, he had just turned into a narrow alley nearby when a bicycle swooped in from behind and knocked him down.

Charlie fell with a thud, his right leg and arm hitting the stone ground hard enough to suffer immense pain. His already heavy head became intensely dizzy, and blurriness appeared in his vision. He struggled to sit up. Examining himself, he found that his calves, knees, and arms were bloodied now.

The bike wobbled, then steadied. But before Charlie could confront the rider, he had escaped. The rider was a teenage boy. As he grabbed hold of the bike again and flew away, he turned back once to look at Charlie but rushed on, leaving Charlie alone, injured and abandoned on the unknown streets.

Trying to gain control over his blurring pain, he scanned his surroundings. Sporadically people rushed past him in panic, and no one paid any attention to him.

He endured the pain, stood up, and limped forward, although totally ignorant of the situation ahead.

He knew he needed help.

He advanced about 100 meters and all the noises died down.

The alley was quiet.

The commotion in the distance could no longer be heard. It felt like an isolated world cut off from the rest.

His mind was congested with questions, but he somehow managed to calm down.

His eyes switched to the buildings lining the alley.

Behind the walls with fading colors, old bungalow houses, worn but standing tall, lined up on both sides of the alley.

Old gray brick or stucco walls, Chinese temple-style carbon-colored tiled roofs and eaves decorated the pathway. A crimson door under the eaves nearby was shut closed. In front of the door were three stairs with one moderate stone lion squatting on each side. A few bicycles were parked randomly by the wall.

As he walked further, a mature locust tree leaned against the wall, stretching its twisted branches to the sky, forming a lush green canopy of leaves, speaking of an early summer.

The mottled silhouette of the locust tree reflected in Charlie's eyes and the slanting sunlight enlarged its shadow, drowning nearly half of the wall in soothing darkness. It was strangely overwhelming and serene.

Charlie's body was still in pain, but for a brief minute, an inexplicable warmth flooded into his heart.

A tip-tap of approaching footsteps broke Charlie's attention.

He turned his head and saw *her*.

A4

S he slowly walked towards him, her footsteps soft and quiet.

The dark, quiet alley shone in her presence.

Charlie had never seen such a fresh, clean, and expressive face. The word 'beautiful' would be too superficial for it, although accurate. It was a rare kind of beauty that glowed from within the soul.

The concern in her eyes touched Charlie, but there was a shyness to it; a hesitation, a struggle to approach a stranger.

Their eyes met, and in that instant, it felt like a nuclear collision.

She was briefly lost, and turned her face away, now cast in red, to avoid his eyes.

Charlie gazed at her, taking the opportunity to read more into her. She was wearing a hazy blue pencil skirt and a cream-colored summer top that loosely hugged her curves. On her chest was a little, delicate butterfly hanging on a silver necklace. Her hair, silky black, was laid down on her neck in a ponytail.

"You are hurt." She spoke in English in a low, concerned voice. Her eyes had returned to him with assumed composure.

"Yes." He smiled and glanced down at himself, embarrassed.

"I'll go call a cab. You need to go to the hospital." She spoke quickly and was about to turn to leave.

Charlie could not think of anything to say. He was about to thank her, but suddenly everything came back to him and all he could think of was his sudden arrival at this strange, unknown place, and the riot that he had just experienced on the street.

"Wait a sec. I probably won't need to go to the hospital. Just some scrapes and bruises." He blurted out and smiled wryly.

She looked straight into his eyes. Charlie could feel her trying to process the situation.

"Come to my house. My Grandma is also home. Just a short distance ahead." She eventually offered.

The girl led Charlie through the quiet alley, turning into a cozy street, and eventually into a private courtyard.

"Nainai!" She called out in a raised voice in Chinese as she shut the door.

The entrance of the bungalow house inside the yard creaked open, and a tall, thin old woman walked out, her steps measured and wobbly. Clad in a clean gray blouse with her hair tightly pulled in a bun at the back of her head, the old woman eyed him inquisitively; her eyes—bright and spirited, despite her age.

The girl immediately said something to her Grandma, in an apparent attempt to clarify the situation.

Grandma took a cautious look at Charlie and asked the girl something. The girl replied while already guiding Charlie into the house.

It all happened like an unreal dream. Led by both into a well-maintained room inside, Charlie was placed on a bed, where he could sit up against the pillows. The room had minimal furniture—a bed, a few bookshelves, a desk, and an almirah, but it was warm and comfortable.

The girl brought in warm water in a porcelain basin, prepared clean white towels, antiseptic, gauze, etc., and sat down by the bedside. She took one look at Charlie's wounds and began to carefully clean up his bruised leg and arm.

Her fair face still had that ethereal glow he couldn't describe.

She was busy with her operation, paying full attention to making sure every single detail was meticulously executed. She looked up to check on him from time to time, worrying about his pain. There was something hidden in her eyes as she looked up at Charlie; the hesitation, the shyness.

Charlie did not know why he felt so naturally drawn to her like she was his gravity. Perhaps they had been in love in the past. And that right now, the God of Fate had somehow summoned her to rescue him.

He gazed at her, wondering how he could have such a ridiculous idea. His mind was in a whirl. He had completely forgotten about Jennifer, the girls, and the bubble, and now sitting in this house seemed all too miraculous to him. *Is this all real?*

As the girl worked on his arm, Charlie gazed behind her, taking in further details of the room. By the wall behind her were a row of tall bookshelves and a desk on which a few pieces of intriguing Chinese crafts were displayed. Above the desk on the wall was a piece of French painting of a river and some shadowy trees bathed in sunset.

Grandma exchanged a few words with the girl and left.

The room suddenly fell into silence. The air grew heavier, heavier with the breath of the two. Charlie stared at the girl with his unbroken gaze until an indescribable tenderness and hazy desire began brewing in his heart.

But she seemed to be afraid of this silence. She buried her head deep in her nursing work, not once looking up at Charlie; her dexterous fingers moving over his wounds with precision.

He was trying to hold back his pain and attempt a conversation with her.

"Thank you so much for helping me. I'm Charlie." Charlie leaned slightly towards her and spoke.

"Of course. You're welcome. I'm Yinyi." She raised her eyes to briefly meet his, with a soft smile that instantaneously melted Charlie's heart.

Yinyi...

For an unexplainable reason the name echoed warmly in Charlie's subconscious as it tugged at his heartstrings. It was as if a light was suddenly cast on a deeply buried sweet memory although he was unable to recall it.

"Would you mind telling me, *where are we?*" Charlie asked cautiously, trying not to sound too ridiculous.

Yinyi paused her hands briefly, a bit surprised by his question. "We're not too far from Tiananmen Square. You're new in Beijing?"

"*Beijing?!*" Charlie was shocked. "I'm totally lost. It might sound crazy, but, I'm from Louisiana, the United States. I have no clue why I'm here, in *Beijing*. I can't really explain it, if you forgive me." He confessed to her his bafflement, although not expecting it to make any sense to her.

Yinyi seemed briefly perplexed by his response.

"That's ok. You're here. You don't have to explain anything." She said softly, attempting to comfort him.

Charlie held his thoughtful gaze on her face. She knew nothing about what had happened, and yet, her words put him at ease. They calmed him down.

He wanted to embrace this moment, with *her*.

"You're in college?" He asked.

"Yes. But graduating soon, next year."

"You speak English very well."

"Thanks. I'm preparing for the TOEFL English test. I want to go to the US for graduate school. But it's been a little chaotic lately. I don't know what will happen." Yinyi's brows curved in a furrow.

"What's happening?" He was curious.

"Students are protesting against the corruption. They are going on hunger strikes and parades, demanding direct talks with the national leaders. People from all over the country are gathering in Beijing. The situation here is not good. It escalated out of the authority's hands pretty quickly. All the transportation and supply chains are about to collapse any time."

"It sounds pretty crazy." Charlie said. He realized that how little that he had known about China. The mysterious China in turmoil behind its closer door. He had hardly seen any news about it, like Cuba.

"Good thing you escaped. It's really chaotic out there." She paused her treatment again and looked up at him with a subtle smile tugging at her lips.

He smiled back at her and remembered his own time as a college student. "I had also participated in a massive anti-government demonstration in the United States. I was a college student at the time and did not really know what I was doing."

They continued talking to each other, a note of casualness now settling in their voices.

"My parents just returned to their hometown in the north for a funeral. An uncle of mine had died of cancer." She continued. "I'm lucky. My parents always encourage me to go anywhere to pursue my dream, even though I'm a girl, and their only child. My mom prepared US dollars to pay for my tests as soon as she learned that I plan to go to school in the US."

"You're so brave, to go alone to a foreign country. I hardly see any Chinese in the States, now I think about it. Wait, except for three Wang brothers who have built a very successful restaurant business in Louisiana. They work really hard. I mean, *really really* hard."

"*Really?!*" She looked a bit baffled. "Maybe not in Louisiana. But I know a lot of people going there, a few from my college."

Either way, the thought that Yinyi would come to the States excited Charlie. "You have to let me know once you are in the US." He suggested enthusiastically.

"Absolutely." She smiled.

His eyes wandered and paused on the bookshelves behind her. "You have lots of books." He commented.

"Yes. I love those Western classics. I read so many of them. But, I will be a biochemist." she replied. "Genetics is fascinating." Her eyes glowed with enthusiasm.

"Yes." He agreed. "There was a new biotech company in the news the other day. They make insulin from genetically engineered bacteria. It's amazing."

"Oh, I was not aware of that. There seems to be a lot going on outside this place. I can't wait to learn." Yinyi responded as she finished cleaning him and began to apply the antibiotic cream and bandages.

Charlie turned his eyes to a navy-blue porcelain bowl sitting on a nightstand. There was water and a pale pink flower floating in it.

"It's a beautiful flower." He looked at the flower closely and remarked.

"It's a begonia flower." She followed his eyes and explained. "It may sound silly, but I picked it up from the ground. I thought it might last longer if it's kept soaked in water. I have no clue though." She blushed a bit.

"I really like it. It looks so alive. " He said, glancing back at her face. The petals looked like the shade of Yinyi's blushed cheeks, he thought to himself.

Their eyes were locked together. And this time, she did not avert her eyes. She greeted his gaze with the same hidden longing, like something had woken up between them. Something deep, and intense.

She fell silent for a moment. Then she turned toward the nightstand, and leaned over to pick up the flower from the bowl. She handed it over to him.

"This is for you, as a souvenir." She said tenderly.

"Thank you." He accepted it, with a sexy and almost irresistible smile.

He reached into a pocket of his shorts, pulled out a small purse, carefully tucked the flower in, and put it away.

Yinyi's fingers seemed to move slower now. Her treatment was about to be completed but it seemed as if she was unwilling to end it.

Silence again prevailed around them.

He had absolutely no idea what to do next. All he wanted was time to freeze up in this moment.

He wished never to go forward. He wanted to stay here, in the presence of Yinyi. *Forever.*

His eyes were suddenly drawn to a Chinese newspaper spread on the bed beside him. His frown deepened as he continued to stare at it.

She followed his eyes to the newspaper, and back to him, not understanding what was going on.

"*Is this today's date?!*" Charlie grabbed the newspaper with his free hand, reading it more closely. Putting it down in front of Yinyi, he pointed to the top left corner of the front page.

She didn't expect him to be able to read Chinese.

Yinyi took a look. "That's right. May 30."

"You mean May 30, *1989.*"

"Yes."

Charlie's realization struck back with a blow. *He had gone to China in 1989.*

He stared at Yinyi blankly and instantly remembered Nassau Island and the Love Beach.

And the gigantic bubble.

The Bubble.

His head exploded at such realization and his emotions instantaneously went on a roller coaster ride. Initially the shock and excitement that *he had just time travelled!* Then the fear of being stranded in China in a different time. *How would he survive? Can he make it back to where he was?!* And the tender thought of Yinyi and his feelings towards her.

Yinyi was not even in his own time!

How could it be?!

Charlie felt a sudden surge of indescribable emotions inside him. He gazed at her, wanting to preserve all the details of her face in his memory; he was determined to make sure that she was indeed, *real.*

He saw the desire in her eyes that had been ignited by him, the lingering affection and the helpless struggle that passed in that beautiful heart of hers.

And suddenly something else in his subconscious awakened quietly.

A beam of light passed through the dark abyss of his memory.

That white beam hit Charlie this time and he desperately grabbed her hand.

"Yinyi, we have met before."

He murmured.

A5

“Charlie!”

A vague female voice woke him up from his reverie. Jennifer was calling for him.

Everything in front of him disappeared instantaneously and he was again back in the waters of Nassau Island.

Like awakening from a dream, he realized that his body had fully recovered. Or more precisely, it remained the same as before.

With powerful strokes, he began to swim upwards until finally his face emerged from the water.

The glowing sun rays drenched him, and he took a deep breath under the dazzling blue sky.

Jennifer was not far ahead, looking back at him. Her long brown hair, now wet, was clinging to her face as she bobbed on the waves.

Charlie cruised through the sea, following Jennifer to the shore. Once on solid ground, he examined his body carefully, looking up and down his arms and legs. Not one scar or bruise could be found. He pinched himself on the arm and confirmed that tactile pain was still there.

He stopped and stared blankly out at the sea.

His brain was a mess as if it had been desolated by a hurricane. He was unable to think.

He tried to digest all the bizarre things that had just happened.

The scenes kept replaying themselves mechanically and uncontrollably in his mind. *Was he hallucinating? What just happened?*

It felt like a dream from which he had awoken. But it felt real and emotionally intense.

The feelings toward the girl, Yinyi, were still there. His entire being urged him to go back to her, to China in 1989. His thoughts intensified, and he couldn't help himself.

He wondered if she really existed, perhaps in some parallel universe.

How strange that she felt like a black hole which had been hidden deep for a long time in his consciousness, a black hole filled with the unknowns. There buried was a past that he could neither touch nor recall.

Everything around him seemed so detached. The sun was still shining lavishly, and the sea was sparkling. It was quiet and warm on the beach, except for the low roar of the tides. Jennifer was busy with the two girls, playing and screaming on the beach. Only Charlie seemed to be pulled between the extremes of his reality and dream.

Unbelievable!

He forced himself to calm down. He brainstormed over what could have happened but every turn he took, he could find no reason to believe that it was a hallucination.

He suddenly remembered something and rushed to reach out into the pocket of his shorts. He pulled out the wallet that had been kept safely in a plastic zip-lock bag.

He opened the wallet and found a carefully folded *begonia flower.*

A6

To the northeast of the town of Hammond, Louisiana, laid an area of approximately 23 acres of green grassy land. A large grove of ancient pine and oak trees enveloped the area in a lush shade against the sky. Nestled inside was a six-acre Mirror Lake, adding to the beauty of the quiet and cool park. Further decorated with colorful flowers and short bridges over winding creeks, the luxurious park was a favorite for all who visited.

The property had a lot of history and was known as the Zemmuray Garden.

The former house owner had hired a prominent New Orleans architect named Moise Goldstein to design the adjacent house and gardens. Since then, it became famous, inviting and alluring tourists every year to see the flowers bloom in spring.

Except for that, no one knew the new owner of the luscious garden, the young millionaire, *Charlie O'Connell.*

Charlie had only one full-time housekeeper, Mr. Montgomery, a tall and thin man with a slightly lame left leg, to take care of the property, and a crew of part-time workers to help in the gardens.

Mr. Montgomery used to run a shop for Charlie's Dad. During that time Montgomery's mother was struggling with late-stage lung cancer. Montgomery was burdened by the mounting medical bills and nearly bankrupted. Charlie's father offered help as soon as he learned about it. He found the lady the best specialist in the area and covered all her expenses.

The lady lived on for two more years than the doctors had predicted. Before she passed away, she made her son promise to serve Charlie's family for the rest of his life.

It was a special friendship reciprocated by gratitude.

Therefore, it came as no surprise that when Charlie sold his father's business and let go of all the staff, Mr. Montgomery insisted on staying, no matter what he would be asked to do. Charlie had no choice but to keep him as his housekeeper.

One early morning, Charlie returned home after his morning jogs in the garden as usual. His routine constituted a shower after exercise followed by drinking milk in the dining room and reading the newspaper that Mr. Montgomery had picked up.

That afternoon, Jennifer showed up unexpectedly at his house. Only after a few words, they found themselves in his bedroom.

Keeping a sultry gaze on Charlie, Jennifer was beginning to undress when she caught a glimpse of a new addition to the wall.

A wilted begonia flower was carefully framed. The edges of the petals had begun to curl up and looked a bit rusty.

"What's this?" She asked.

"Oh, a gift from a friend." He replied vaguely, busy removing his own apparel.

Out of curiosity she moved closer to look and was about to reach out and take it down.

"Don't touch!" He shouted abruptly.

He immediately stepped over and stood between her and the wall.

"Don't touch it." He stared at her and repeated in a grave manner.

"Why?" She asked casually, her fingers gently picking open the white shirt he had just unbuttoned and stroking his naked chest provocatively.

"Because, because it does not belong to this world." Charlie moved away.

She pouted in disapproval. Another crazy talk from Charlie that made no sense to her.

Jennifer Sanchez was half Italian and half Mexican, and two years older than Charlie. She had just gotten divorced when they met for the first time at their mutual friend *Doug Smith*'s house party. Doug had inherited his father's business that dominated the local restaurant supplies. He and Charlie had been friends for years.

Wearing a blood-red dress that flattered her curvy body and swaying her hips on a pair of high heels, Jennifer had turned everyone's head the moment she showed up at the party.

But Charlie was not one who would go around pleasing girls. He hung out with Doug with a nonchalant look, drinking beer and laughing in the shade of an old oak tree in the backyard.

The smell of the charcoal fire and meaty aroma of the barbecue filled the evening air. It was still hot and humid with no breeze in early September. The sultry heat of the late summer led to constant sweat, as if invisible microbes had densely populated the skin, blocking all the pores. The body felt stagnant, unable to breathe, and blood was struggling to flow.

Lots of people crowded inside and outside the house—drinking a variety of wines, shouting out, and laughing loudly. Indulged in intoxication and enjoying the blurred state between life and death, everyone was venting out the vitality that had accumulated throughout the summer and had nowhere to go.

Jennifer's alluring bright red figure fluttered in the crowd like a butterfly. Shortly, the butterfly landed in front of Charlie and Doug. She leaned in, greeted Doug warmly, and chatted a little about the car she'd just fixed, but her intoxicated eyes kept drifting to Charlie irresistibly.

He noticed the desire in her eyes.

She requested his help to get to the car and carry a case of beer. Then, exaggeratedly swinging her hips, she led him out of the noisy yard and onto the street.

The streets were empty and quiet. The trees on both sides were bathed in the last touch of the disappearing golden sunlight, casting mottled shadows on the ground that seemed to be motionless.

She stopped in front of a black Chevy on the side of the road, opened the trunk of the car and leaned in.

Her long silky hair flowed down her back. The thin fabric of the skirt was stained with the fine sweat on her body and clung to her hips. Her legs stood erect; strained with desire and tension.

She reached out and rummaged inside.

"Oh, what happened? I was sure I had it." She muttered pretentiously with a wicked smile hanging on her lips.

From his position behind her, Charlie could easily tell that the trunk was empty with nothing but a couple of shirts.

She suddenly turned around, raised her head, and fixed her eyes straight at him.

Charlie stood unfazed, his eyes roaming over her eager face. His beautiful brown-green eyes seemed to have seen through her long ago but still carried a rather innocent focus, as well as a bewilderment that wavered on the edge of desire.

"Must have left it at home. You have to come with me." She turned her head abruptly to avoid his gaze and murmured.

It should have been an accidental one-night stand for them. But things got more complicated on the way. A few days later, Charlie was going to take another girl out on a date as planned originally. There was never a shortage of girls around him. As he and his date were just about to walk into the cinema, Jennifer unexpectedly appeared with a long face in front of them on the street.

Charlie found himself in a conflicting situation. He was embarrassed, not knowing how she had found out his whereabouts.

Under the streetlamp, she confronted him. It was as if there was a dark substance being awakened in her body, gloomy and unpredictable, echoing the thick night behind her, and brewing a thunderstorm.

"I am not used to men whom I've dated, taking other women out on dates." She said bitterly.

He sensed the unhappiness and anger hidden in her voice. Feeling embarrassed, he hesitated for a moment, and attempted a compromise. "I will go to your place after the movie with her," he replied.

Jennifer nodded and agreed.

That was how Charlie ended up being stuck with Jennifer.

Though he entertained her physical endeavors, he always kept a subtle distance from her. She could come to see him, but she was rarely invited to sleep in. He said he was not used to having someone around when he tried to fall asleep.

He took her to concerts and bars. They caught everyone's eyes and were welcomed everywhere they went as a good-looking couple. But Charlie always turned a deaf ear to her talks of moving in together or getting married.

It seemed that her possession of him was only a shadow, a sexy and handsome shadow, and a shadow that satisfied her vanity, a shadow confirming that she could never have the *real* Charlie. The shadow always drifted away at any moment and threatened to disappear into the night, beyond her reach.

At this moment, while he stared at the withered Begonia flower, deep in thought, she knew she had lost him again.

That evening, Charlie and Jennifer drove out of town to the old Napoleon House, a poplar bar in New Orleans.

It was dimly lit inside, and the old, freckled walls were covered with photographs of Napoleon—his single pictures, pictures will his officials, and pictures of his famous mustached countenance.

Jennifer held Charlie's arm and walked straight to the front desk of mahogany as if no one else was present.

He pulled his arm from her, glancing at the Napoleon statues and piles of exotic wine bottles lined behind the bartender.

"Two glasses of Old Fashioned." He said to the middle-aged bartender behind the counter, who was wearing a short-sleeved white shirt and a bow tie.

The wine slowly dissipated in his body, bringing out the sensation of melting ice or snow that was both warm and burning.

Two local acquaintances approached them and chatted about Harry Connick Jr's upcoming music tour in New Orleans. At the end of the conversation, they patted Charlie affectionately on the shoulder and left.

Sipping on his wine, Charlie's eyes fell on a painting on the wall, of a soldier behind Napoleon.

He looks a lot like Bill, Charlie thought to himself.

A7

Charlie hadn't remembered *Bill Segal* in a long time. Looking at the picture, he realized how much he missed the intellectual bond he had shared with Bill.

It all began with their childhood friendship. Two teenagers with extraordinary intelligence found themselves hanging out together, talking about science and fantasizing about the universe and interstellar space.

They spent hours in the guest house in Charlie's parent's spacious backyard. It was their secret hideout filled with all sorts of electronic parts, electronic telescopes for astronomical observations, and containers with odd samples. Behind the guest house was a pine forest that hosted all kinds of birds that came for the season, chirping and singing their days away.

Charlie's family was wealthy. His father owned several electronic stores, and the business was booming. Charlie was not a quiet, disciplined child. He had taken apart many appliances in the stores, getting nearly whipped by his strict German mother, despite being their only child.

His father was in his forties when Charlie was born.

Father was, however, reluctant to discipline Charlie. For him, his child's interest in his wares excited him the most.

His father's family background had remained a mystery; no one had ever seen any relatives from his side. With a touch of aristocracy and an English accent, he had showed up in this small town, in Louisiana, by himself, settled down, got married, had a kid, and said nothing about his past.

Bill was a more mild-natured boy with a freckled face, not as wild and reckless as Charlie. He came from a large family of five children where his parents always juggled part-time jobs to make a living, always being stretched thin between them.

Bill and Charlie had become so intellectually close that Bill often stayed back at Charlie's house for dinner. He loved the delicious blueberry pies prepared by Charlie's mother.

In contrast to Charlie's caprice and destructiveness, Bill was quiet and disciplined. He loved math, chemistry, and logical reasoning in all theories. He always drew formulas and cartoon symbols on the whiteboard on the wall of Charlie's guest house and the two of them would sit about, improving their drawings and symbols.

But their passion for science was driven only by natural curiosity instead of a purpose. Rather, their scientific experiments and discussions allowed them to pull all kinds of pranks that their intelligent brains could generate.

They would ignite cherry bombs and throw them into the cylinders of the road sewers, just to hear the sound of their blasting, in waves, which traveled a few blocks away.

When no one was around, they would push the tires piled up at the Firestone store down a steep slope in the small town and watch them roll all the way down to the lower entrance of the Columbus Cinema.

Their only fright was situated in one figure. As soon as the slow figure of Mrs. Bright, the theatre manager, emerged, the boys would run away and hide in Charlie's guest house. They didn't know why they feared her, but her presence would be the end of all their experiments.

Charlie was 12 years old. Bill was 14.

These old events buried in his memory years ago rose like revived geothermal bubbles. With all the bubbles, arose one that spoke of *that night.*

How could he forget that starry night!

It was hot in the guest house and the door was left half-open.

Charlie and Bill were busy drawing an imaginary time travel machine on the whiteboard: its electromagnetically driven wings, and how it could break free from the gravity of the planets.

They decided its route to be along the trajectory of the Earth's rotation, but slowly reversed.

Like a reversed shadow.

Maybe antimatter, antiparticle.

There was always such a possibility.

Just like the eyes looked from the inside out, following the same visual pathway, vision could be reversed, and one could look into the inside from the outside.

Bill finished speaking, polished off an iced Coke, and slammed the empty bottle on the pinewood table.

As the thud of the glass echoed in the silence, the door suddenly swung open, accompanied by a man's painful moan.

The boys turned to look in shock.

The man holding, or rather, leaning on the door was dressed as a British soldier with red robes and white trousers, and a bunch of feathers on his hat. He bent over and covered his abdomen, his face sallow, drenched in cold sweat.

"*Help!*" He cried out in a whispering broken voice.

Charlie heard, and instinctively leaned forward, and was about to step toward the soldier when Bill stopped him.

"Yellow fever." Bill stared at the soldier and whispered nervously.

The boys slowly backed off.

The soldier raised his head, his eyes red with pain but no emotions playing on his face. He stared at them for a while and abruptly vanished.

The boys stood, frozen in horror, exchanging quiet glances. They slowly and cautiously tiptoed to the door and peeked out, examining the surroundings. The quiet pine forest was shrouded in starry lights, casting dense shadows on the ground.

In the dark, invisible ghosts seemed to be gathering, looming about, ready to pounce on them at any moment.

Fear, as potent as lightning, seized them again.

Without saying a word, they fled frantically to Charlie's parents' main house.

The event ended up being his and Bill's secret forever. No one else believed them.

On that sweltering night, Charlie and Bill shivered uncontrollably in fear.

As soon as Charlie's dad had the entire story, he got up immediately, pulled out a gun from the closet, loaded it up, and went out to check the pine woods.

After several rounds of careful inspection, Dad came back to the house, sat back on the sofa, and continued reading his newspaper; his countenance betraying no emotions.

Charlie's mom made chicken soup for them, and said in disbelief, "Where are those crazy ideas coming from? Charlie, you're spending too much time fooling around. You'd better learn to behave."

Such an important, unusual event was left simply ignored, by everyone. Maybe the parental interest was limited exclusively to confirming its absurdity, not its existence or reason. The unknown is always disturbing, even terrifying, and it is of no use to invoke that in a happy life in this world. Charlie's parents chose to deny it. To exclude it was the most natural disposition.

But Charlie and Bill could never forget. They did not have to dig too deep into the history to discover that there was indeed a war between the United States and Britain in 1815, five miles away from New Orleans. At that time, the British army had suffered heavy losses. Nearly 300 soldiers were killed, and almost 500 were missing or captured.

It was quite plausible now that this could have served as an explanation for the appearance of the English soldier they had encountered.

But the soldier had very strangely appeared at the very moment the two teenagers were fantasizing about time travel. Assuming this was indeed the case, all the odd happenings seemed to be a corroboration, suggesting that time may not be a rigid straight line, but a tangled mess, inadvertently dislocated and crossed. The British soldier with the yellow fever might have gotten lost inadvertently in the space of time and arrived at the wrong interface.

A similar coincidence could be claimed by those, who, while communicating with the dead, awakened the dead at the very moment of their pretentious ritual. Evidence of those coincidences was dubious and convenient. Who could guarantee that Charlie and Bill weren't seeing the British soldier in their hallucination? This possibility terrified them even more, as it suggested the fragility and limitations of their own physical perception—the only basis that humans possess, on which the entire understanding of the world is built.

The frequency of their visits to the guesthouse eventually died down. That incident had left enough impact on the two minds to keep them away from the spot of all their confusion. In fear and uncertainty, their two years of a good time in the guest house ended and years later Bill moved out eventually to Florida for college.

A8

When Charlie met Bill again, it was at Charlie's father's funeral.

Years had passed and his father had just turned 65. Having amassed a large sum of money, he was planning to retire and enjoy his old age in relaxation. Since Charlie had no interest in taking over the family business, Dad had started looking for a buyer.

It had started out as an ordinary morning.

Mom was frying fresh bacon and eggs purchased from a friend's farm. She was gossiping about her friend's house while taking out the freshly baked sourdough bread, filling the entire kitchen with the tempting aroma of bread.

A wisp of early morning sun sifted through the verdant pine forest in the backyard and reflected inside through the glass door. The green grass was still wet with the morning dew.

Not far away, a garbage collection truck ran over the road, making a throbbing noise.

Dad was talking to a yard guy in the back of the property. All seemed to be following the usual morning routine. But all of a sudden, Dad slammed open the kitchen door, clutching his stomach. Sweat beaded all over his forehead; his face twisted in pain.

Dad was immediately rushed to the hospital early in the morning and was placed in the operating room under general anesthesia for routine gastroscopy. A few hours later Mom called Charlie. She could barely hold herself. She informed him that Dad had died on the operating table.

That was the year when Charlie had turned nineteen, a freshman at Yale.

Dad was buried outside the town in the family cemetery that he had bought long ago. A few thin trees guarded it nearby, beyond which, was an open wild field. The field was immense, thus a perfect setting for the lingering spirits of the dead.

The grief of his father pulled Charlie deep into utter emptiness. At first, the anguish seemed like an almost instinctive reaction. His consciousness was completely hollowed out by the loss.

At the funeral, Charlie was nothing more than a living puppet guided by his mother—acknowledging the people who were trying to comfort them. But everything around him happened to be a mum movie, playing away at its own pace. Within, he was completely devastated by his father's sudden death. He had been at a loss as to how to accept it or move on from it.

Bill stayed with Charlie for a few days after the funeral. One day they stood in front of Charlie's father's tombstone. Charlie gently put down a bouquet on the tomb.

Standing for a while in silence, Charlie and Bill slowly walked towards a nearby café. Once settled inside the café, through the window, they watched people pass by on the street.

"Dad worked hard his *entire* life. Never rested or gave any time for pleasure. *Never.* The only rest he had was to watch the news and read the paper. He didn't even get to enjoy a single day of retirement." As Charlie broke the silence to reflect on his dad's life, his broken voice came out in a shattered lament.

"Life is short and unpredictable," sighed Bill.

As Charlie and Bill sat, chatting in the café, the humming of a multitude sounds filled Charlie's head—the hiss of the coffee machine, the murmurings of the occupants of the other tables, and the slow slurping of coffee. But dulling these sounds were the empty blackness and silence in Charlie's head which kept drifting back, pulling him deeper into his agony.

The shockwave inside him started to fade away, but the agony of the initial grief started to settle deeper inside him. Realization befell him and he found himself still standing there, facing the empty world, left behind by Dad.

Everything seemed to have lost the warmth they had had in the past. All was irrelevant and emotionless.

It felt that he was simply a shadow accidentally projected into the scene, a meaningless shadow, a virtual shadow, a shadow of a walking dead himself.

The entire world, busy with its own business, suddenly seemed to lose its weight and direction. It lost its temperature and its color and was completely disconnected from his joy or sorrow.

It was like a solitary abandoned straw hat, simply floating randomly and purposelessly in the nothingness of the empty and cold universe.

Nothingness was everywhere and everything brought on nothing but despair.

Charlie felt himself slowly sliding off to the final edge of the straw hat at this moment, and if he went just a little bit further, he would merge into the large virtual, becoming one with the nothingness.

He turned his head, scanning all the living beings around him. He couldn't connect with their hustle and bustle and their happiness. It seemed to be just a visual phenomenon, a flat and thin visual that was separated from him by a thick layer of frosted glass wall.

He couldn't hear any sound. It played out in front of his eyes like a silent black-and-white movie on the screen and he was the only audience in a desolate cinema.

It was the emptiness that he had never felt before, as if someone had punched huge holes of voids within him.

It was an emptiness filled with loneliness. It was the emptiness that sucked away his breath, making it hard for him to survive.

The emptiness was like being stranded on the lonely side of the river and cursed with the bane of standing alone and watching the happiness of people; not being able to cross over to the other side.

The emptiness of white snow covering the enormous expanse of the Earth, and the emptiness of epiphany that was followed with neither thought nor desire.

"It is so true that one cannot bring wealth with him at birth or upon death. It's not really worth consuming one's entire life for it. I'll never do what Dad did."

"You still don't want to take over his business." Bill looked at him thoughtfully.

"No, I don't. If Mom allows it, I will sell the asset, and turn it over to an investment firm just to cover the living expenses," said Charlie.

"I won't put off happiness like Dad." Charlie spoke in a blank voice. "I'd rather enjoy life while I'm still alive."

"Charlie." Bill glanced at him, hesitating.

"*What is it?*" Charlie stared into Bill's eyes. He felt as if he already knew what was on Bill's mind. It was the memory that they were both deliberately avoiding but which always came back to haunt them from the past.

"Something happened last year." Bill finally confessed. "I was scuba diving with a female friend in Florida. It's *not* a girlfriend I'm talking of."

Charlie knew Bill's reservation when it came to girls. Throughout their teenage Bill had never dated anyone, nor did he have any crush on anyone.

"We had just finished our exams and couldn't wait to have some fun. It was a clear day. The boat set out from the east coast. It dropped us off near the shore.

Everything went well in the beginning. We swam by schools of colorful fish. We spotted clusters of coral at the shallow bottom of the ocean. Absolutely amazing. But soon we found ourselves stranded in dim underwater caves. No one had said anything about the caves. They were steep and ferocious, with a few stalactites hanging down. They were apparently connected and started to emerge from left and right, one after another. We panicked and soon got separated. I lost my way completely. In the end, I was lucky enough to stumble out of the caves and return to the boat.

But I couldn't find the girl. She had not returned to the boat.

We waited for the girl on the boat for a while. The instructors went down into the ocean to search for her. But in the end, she was nowhere to be found."

Bill's eyes showed the enormous sadness that he desperately tried to hide.

"Charlie, I am often reminded of those mathematical formulae we used to write, formulae about the universe. Physics needs to be verified, but verification requires conditions and means of detection, which are limited by our own scientific equipment capabilities.

But math is different. It can let our imagination run wild, revealing all logical possibilities and secrets.

Not simple one-dimensional math. I am talking about mathematics that's as complex, dynamic, evolving, and fascinating as life itself.

Abstract mathematics.

Organic mathematics.

Mathematics that can give machines souls and minds. Mathematics that can explain the secrets of space and time.

That's right. *The secret of time and space!*

The moment we saw the British soldier at your guest house seven years ago, I knew there was something, *a concealed secret* behind the whorls of time and space."

"Charlie." Bill stared at Charlie, a strange flame burning in his eyes.

"Do you know why I chose to go to Florida? Big scholarships were important, of course. But have you ever thought about it? *The Bermuda Triangle is right there. Miami is part of the triangle. It is that close.*

I wonder what happened to those planes and ships that disappeared for no reason. *What is the secret of the Bermuda Triangle?*

Charlie, is it possible that they simply crossed our world and went to another universe like the planes and ships that vanished and that is why we can't see them? *Is it possible that maybe, just maybe, they simply went somewhere else?*

I want to find that secret Charlie. That secret of time and space."

A9

In the bar, Charlie's eyes were glued to the picture on the wall.

Napolean was facing the sea, defeated for the last time. He was standing on a French battleship, reflecting on the mishaps of fate. Worry and fear played clearly on the faces of the soldiers behind him.

But one looked different from the rest of the soldiers. He stood a bit further away and was instead looking slightly down with his hat in his hands. With his curly hair and freckled face, *he looked exactly like Bill.*

Bill had confirmed that at least fifty ships and twenty planes had disappeared mysteriously in the Bermuda Triangle, without a distress signal, leaving no wreckage.

He had combed through all the reported incidents, including the USS Cyclops, which disappeared there in 1911.

Was it a Rogue Wave—an anomaly in the magnetic environment, *or something else unknown?!*

Bill's curiosity made him travel to Bermuda for his summer break. However, his entire time there was spent diving, drinking beer, and reading *Hegel's Little Logic.*

Wanting to tour the island a little, Bill rented a bicycle one day, what the locals termed a pedal bike. While riding through busy downtown Hamilton, he encountered an accident. A car had hit him amidst the chaotic traffic, and he was taken to the hospital.

This was where he first met her—*Elizabeth Johnson*, a female student from a medical school in Ontario, Canada. Elizabeth was a volunteer on the island and happened to be assigned to nurse Bill.

His first image of her was the smile on her face. The moment she walked in, it was like the sun shining into the whole room.

She greeted him and arranged for him to take an X-ray. She caught a glimpse of the "*Little Logic*" book lying beside his bed and couldn't help but wonder.

"Your book?"

"Yes. Just to kill time."

"My father is a professor of philosophy. He also has this book. But it's the first time I've seen this book outside his study."

"*Really?!* What a wonderful coincidence!" He could not help but smile.

It was at this moment that a sudden realization struck him. He was attracted to her, enchanted by her smile, her body, and her words. Even though she was wearing the uniform of a local nurse—a white suit loosely wrapped around her grown body and a blue-brimmed white hat, he knew that he had fallen in love for her.

Years later, Bill graduated with a PhD and became a rising star in marine animal research.

Charlie had drifted away with his chain of thoughts as he stared at the picture on the bar wall. When he woke up from his memories, Jennifer was no longer around.

He glanced around and caught a glimpse of her standing in the bar aisle, apparently having a quite engaged conversation with a tall man.

She lifted her face to him, with her curvy body in a tight skirt leaning forward. Charlie could almost see the glow on her face, the flirtatious look he was familiar with.

She was like a lustful female black spider, single-mindedly weaving a web, waiting for a new prey, her singular aim being to mate with the prey and then devour it.

He sighed and turned his eyes away from her. *How did he get stuck with her?!* As he sipped on his drink, the chattering of people and all the other noises receded away like low tides. His consciousness began to float up like bubbles, but his body still felt heavy with gravity.

Strangely, he felt his body giving way to his consciousness to split up into an individual entity.

The floating consciousness became freer and lighter, growing out wings, and soaring up in the air.

It was as if he was having that out-of-body moment again. From the air he looked down at the crowd, the purposeless beings indulging in the pleasure of being lost in drinking, and at his lonely self, aimless, directionless, wasting away in the name of happiness.

He saw Jennifer finally come back to him.

She bounced towards him and told him that she had bumped into an old high school acquaintance who had become an airline pilot and was in New Orleans for a short stay.

Her eyes flashed excitement with the joy of being admired.

He smiled and said, "Great, you should invite him over."

But something changed in her face, and she added coldly, "He just asked me if I was seeing someone. I said *no*."

Charlie's face froze for a moment. He suddenly threw down his glass on the bar counter.

"I'm done here." He got up immediately and strode out of the bar.

The night was dark with only a few stars. With a stiff face, Jennifer followed him into the car.

Charlie didn't say a word and quickly turned the steering wheel.

Jennifer soon started cursing at him, calling him an asshole, saying she had never wanted to come to New Orleans with him.

Her complaints became louder. She shouted that she wanted to get married, but he was only a hopeless playboy.

He frowned. "That's who I am. I do *not* want a marriage. If you're not happy, you're free to leave."

"I can't be distracted fighting with you while I'm driving." He added and fell back into silence.

The situation didn't follow the script Jennifer had secretly plotted. She had hoped that by showing him she wasn't short of suitors, he would be pressured into a commitment.

After all, her goal was to marry this wild, handsome, and extremely wealthy young man.

But she realized that she had never really had any power over Charlie in their relationship.

He always kept a delicate distance from her, not one inch closer or farther, always lingering at the edge of the relationship.

Any effort she made would instead push him further away. It was like holding sand in her hand—the tighter she held it, the faster it slipped out of her fingers.

As a result, frustration, anger, and eventually desperation showered over Jennifer's mind.

She cursed him with more vicious words.

They left the city of New Orleans on interstate 10 and after about half an hour they began the crawl on the narrow Route 55 between the two large lakes.

It was the Maurepas Lake that Charlie had known for a long time, with its stagnant, turbid waters, dense thickets of tall weeds, and the half-dead trees that were covered with wisps of grey Spanish moss, like the dust willows of death in the caves of hell.

He used to roam around the lake and swamp, driving a small yacht with his friends, spotting alligators.

But at this moment, the entire lake seemed swallowed by the enchanting night. Peace and tranquility settled in Charlie's mind but behind the window, Charlie could still sense their presence, their eerie existence, and the looming danger.

He suddenly felt an indescribable fear, that furious Jennifer was about to do something crazy, the fear that he always had in the back of his mind.

He softened his voice, trying to coax Jennifer from whatever was going on in her head.

"Thank you for coming out with me.

We're both tired. Let me take you home to rest."

She turned her head to the window and was silent for a moment. When she spoke again, it was in a completely changed tone.

"Babe, I am so sorry. Let's forget all this nonsense and start over. *Would you?*" She asked.

"I swear I don't care about other men. I want to be with *you*."

The initial anger leading them to the brink of breakup suddenly turned into a renewed promise for the future. It seemed to be an all too familiar episode between them: a nasty fight breaking out like an unexpected summer storm, which died down with her peace offerings in tears.

He turned to look at her and his heart softened. He nodded his head in a yes. The silence and calm prevailed till he stopped the car in front of her house.

Her body was a little stiff. She didn't move, as if expecting something.

But he remained motionless as if he did not understand her.

"Good night, Jen." He spoke.

A10

Charlie needed some time alone.

He had remained committed to Jennifer for a few years now, despite their fights. At first, he had hoped that things would smoothen out. But the eventual repetition of the same routine again and again exhausted all hopes.

Jennifer's jealousy was like a gigantic spark that was ready to land on anything and turn it into a destructive fire.

A fight would be triggered by any girl he bumped into if he stopped and chatted with the girl a little longer, or if he chose not to take Jennifer out to a particular place to eat, though they were going out to bars and restaurants for most of their dates, or if he left on the spur of the moment to do something without her. Jennifer was eating up his space and time for himself.

She would always come up with a reason out of nothing to blame and curse him. Her mind was filled up with so much insecurity that it spilled out hatred. After showing her fangs and spitting poison on Charlie in every way possible, it was always in the end that she would repent and offer to make love.

It was only during those moments that he was willing to have her and offer himself to her. Physical pleasure became the only and last bond between them, the only way that they were able to communicate with each other, like two primitive animals without a language or soul.

Charlie wasn't quite bothered by the dysfunctional relationship he was stuck in. Perhaps, he was too young, too complete to understand the need to rely on another soul to maintain and replenish.

He was even subconsciously terrified of the possible intrusion of another soul.

As long as Jennifer was blocked away, her venom wouldn't hurt him.

This was the only way that Charlie considered his relationship to be healthy. This extremely superficial relationship was the only way he considered a relationship for himself.

He wondered if he really longed to know true love, to be in tune with love, to truly love someone. At least for now, it didn't seem to matter.

He took his parents as an example—they were a perfectly harmonized couple, loving and merging into one being. But at the same time, they had abandoned their independent and free selves and degenerated into half-beings.

A half-human being who could no longer move on independently without the other and be happy.

Like two trees so hopelessly tangled together. *You in me and I in you. If one fell, the other would be unable to stay standing.*

Those who ended up falling prey to the claws of Love, found a spouse, and started a family at early ages were rather afraid of loneliness and needed to rely on another soul to be complete. They were the ones who needed the provisions of the marriage law to enforce companionship and rid them of their loneliness.

But that wasn't him.

He was stronger, complete. He was good with himself.

Therefore, he was free.

Charlie decided to reinforce that freedom within himself and flew down to Miami, alone, on his small plane, rented a beach house and planned to spend the weekend.

He settled in the house, took a shower, had salad and a burger at a local café, and stepped out to Miami's sandy beach.

Sun was pouring down unobstructed on the blue ocean, reflecting the mirror-like waves hitting the shore.

Not a single bird was in sight. As far as one could see, the beach was filled with people; some leisurely basking in the sun, some making sandcastles, and some playing and running.

Charlie walked down in his T-shirt and swimming shorts, carrying a camera bag pack. Stopping behind the crowd, he set up his tripod and pointed the camera at the ocean.

Leaning over, he looked through the camera window.

The blue ocean in the frame gently tilted and swayed, undulating, echoing the blushing sun and its burning rays.

He seemed to be witnessing himself diving into the ocean.

The sunlight was once again blocked by the water over his head with only thin rays of light filtering through, creating a transparent towering pine forest that enveloped him.

And his body began shrinking.

Shrinking until the bubble appeared.

Until Yinyi appeared.

Yinyi and the begonia flower.

The camera screen magically isolated those queer events from the noisy world.

He zoomed in toward the ocean, patiently adjusting the aperture and speed, as if trying hard enough would allow him to explore that secret spectrum of vision, allow him to see through the ocean, and find the root of all the mysterious events.

He stared for a while, then looked up and pressed the shutter.

The camera was picked up by Charlie in South Korea a few years ago.

The war with Vietnam was persisting at the moment, and Charlie's father had just passed away. Bored with college and trying to find some distraction, Charlie volunteered to enlist in the army on a random whim.

He took a year of boot camp training in El Paso, Texas, and morphed from a charming, carefree youngster into a decisive, independent, strong man.

Shortly, he was dispatched to be with a military base in South Korea for one year.

He found himself stranded in an unnamed small village that he would never find on a map in the future. Poverty was everywhere. It was dusty and connected to the outside world only by a single asphalt road called Military Material Road 1 (MS1). The only other means of contact was the track for the old steam engine trains that ran nearby.

Charlie's special talent in technology landed him in the Technical Equipment unit of the barracks. He spent all his time playing with various instruments and tools and watching a group of soldiers who did nothing but smoke marijuana all day.

One day during their routine rounds, he took a taxi with two other soldiers. As usual, they walked twelve miles from the camp, crossed the Han River, and came to Yongsan, south of Seoul, where he found the shop at the base; it was called PX for short.

The shop wasn't that big. Charlie stopped casually in front of the counter and caught a glimpse of the camera.

A silver metal case, wrapped in black leather, stamped with Ricoh.

He immediately felt a throb in his heart and asked for the camera.

His thoughts flowed over to Mr. James, who was always clothed in a plaid shirt.

In the dimly lit cinema projection room, Mr. James' slightly chubby body leaned against the huge projector, earnestly teaching thirteen-year-old Charlie how to observe the signal of the dot in the upper right corner of the film, and precisely time the switch between two identical projectors.

To his ears, the projectors were always rustling with a mysterious, intriguing, and at the same time monotonous, weary noise.

As the projectors rolled, the dialogues and music in the movie echoed in the huge space of the theater downstairs, as if echoing in an empty, dark valley.

Countless images evolved continuously on the white screen in front of the machine through his and James' hands.

Like magic, it carried the audience in the dark to another world.

It was Charlie's first part-time job. His parents insisted that he learn how to work. Despite being rich, they did not want their child to be spoilt and lack the understanding of work and discipline in life.

Unexpectedly he took considerable pleasure in it.

Charlie's first camera was introduced to him by Mr. James. One day at work, Mr. James came up to him with a camera, showing and explaining the functions and intricacies of the device to Charlie.

With sparks in his eyes, he said, "Charlie, I'll retire one day, and I'll travel the world with it.

There's nothing more fascinating than photography.

Through images, you can find entirely new worlds altogether."

The long stretches of the white sandy beach of Miami spread out in front of Charlie, the rising tide pushing onto the shore, exhausting itself in an exhale, and diminishing completely into the fine sands.

It was nothing out of the ordinary.

Charlie pressed the shutter, then stopped.

He noticed something far into the ocean and frowned slightly.

Two dark shadows emerged in the empty ocean, rising in and out of the tide.

Charlie watched intently. His eyes were removed from the camera screen.

The shadows swept to the shore with the tide, getting closer and bigger. The outlines of the dolphins now came into view.

In the next minute, something incredible happened.

Around the two dolphins that had almost landed on the shore, more and more dolphins suddenly emerged magically, ten, twenty, nearly a hundred, like a massive troop that had been lurking in the distance, now suddenly fell out on the shore.

They were thrown on the beach as if pulled and thrashed by the tides one after another. Their white bellies and gray-black backs laid exposed; their tails fluttering in panic.

In the blink of an eye, the entire coast was covered by a huge school of dolphins flapping and flailing in the shallow water.

Charlie's heart sank. He dropped the camera work and ran over immediately.

He rushed to a dolphin, grabbed its tail, and dragged it forcibly back into the deeper water. The dolphin weighed almost double Charlie's weight. Pulling one back into the water rendered him breathless.

Tourists on the beach gathered, and the men rushed with him. They ran back and forth, hauling the dolphins one by one back to the ocean until the last dolphin entered the water unharmed.

The entire crowd, overwhelmed with joy, now burst into cheers and applauds.

Charlie glanced at the crowd, nodded and smiled, and strode back to his camera.

Standing behind the tripod, Charlie could not get his mind off what had just happened. He found it difficult to go back to his camera work.

He contemplated for a while, packed up the camera, and walked away.

He stopped by a roadside public phone booth, went in, and dialed a number.

"Are you saying that the dolphin's magnetic crystals for navigation could have been messed up?"

"What was the source of the interference?" He asked.

A11

Charlie barely made out the outline of the darkroom under the faint red light glowing in the corner.

It was his specially remodeled darkroom in the villa. Not a single window could be seen in the room. A clock hung on one corner of the wall. On one end of the table were four trays containing solutions. On the other end were paper cutters, amplifiers, and such.

On a clothesline above the table were pictures that were drying.

Charlie skillfully picked up a piece of print paper that had just been exposed on the enlarger and plunged it carefully into the developer, the stop bath, and then the fixer.

The smell of chemicals filled his nostrils.

He stared at the blurry shadows of the print paper, tracking the time till the visuals emerged.

The dark room was like a magic box.

The results of all his hard work would be revealed here, be it good or bad.

The dark room was the place that would reveal all the things that brought him visual pleasure.

Petals of purple orchid backlit by sunlight streaming in from the window.

A row of old-fashioned arches on the streets of New Orleans stretched out to the distant end of the view.

A lonely man lingering alone, looking for companionship.

The face of a sweet seventeen-year-old girl, her face displaying no emotions but looking as natural and fresh as morning dew, full and beautiful.

She was lying down on the rug, her long chestnut hair fanning in thick, shiny waves spreading like a waterfall.

She was a girl he had met briefly. She frequented the local bars, with a body and demeanor almost like a mature woman. Her brother was a shop owner and had introduced her to Charlie. "Can you take her to your place and click some pictures?" he had asked.

Charlie had been baffled by her and her brother's intentions. He treated her as a simple young girl, but she seemed to have already grown out of her presumably innocent age.

She came to his house, posing in different dresses and poses, in a natural goddess-like modeling manner, cold and beautiful.

In between the photographic sessions, her beautiful brown-green eyes would always linger on him. Her eyes deep and meaningful, felt as if they had something to say but were hesitant. It was a paradoxical desire that wandered between pure ignorance and a purpose.

He chose to ignore it and focus on the camera. After one photo session, he stopped seeing her, even though her brother kept suggesting it.

A year later the girl was getting married. Her mother invited Charlie to be her wedding photographer and he saw her again.

On the wedding day, in the shade of a giant old oak tree, she stood next to the groom, receiving blessings from relatives and friends.

The beautiful white dress that she wore added to her charm. Her face was still expressionless yet fresh, full, and glistening. It was as if her natural beauty and vitality were sufficient for her; no effort was needed to add to it.

In the dark room, time became extraordinarily stagnant, frozen in the river of infinity.

His consciousness began to float, suspended in the desolate vacuum of interstellar space. It tried to move forward, but there was absolutely no way.

A vague sense of anxiety clutched onto Charlie, the anxiety that consciousness had nowhere to land itself.

His body seemed to have lost its senses, almost ceasing to exist. And the soul had escaped the body—an empty, wandering nothingness.

His eyes glanced over the wall. He knew there were old pictures left there; old pictures reviving old memories.

He couldn't remember the girl's name. His brief interaction with her was rather visual, artistic, casual, and deliberately kept at a distance by him.

There was no affection or intention. Not even friendship.

All he remembered was her, sitting on the sofa, watching him fiddling with the camera in his hand.

"You will be a great photographer.

You do love it and you are so focused," she had commented.

It was a casual voice, without enthusiasm of offering either a praise or a complaint.

He listened, stopped, and glanced at her.

Wonder and puzzlement approached him. A seventeen-year-old child seemed to be seeing through him completely, but clearly, she knew nothing about him.

The picture of the girl was no longer on the wall. Jennifer was unhappy with it the moment she laid her eyes on it. She had ripped it off the wall during a fight and cut it into pieces with iron scissors in the darkroom.

She called the girl a naturally born little bitch, although the girl had been married to someone else, and had nothing to do with Charlie.

"You are crazy." He had said, staring at her in disbelief.

He couldn't understand why there was so much jealousy in Jennifer. It was like the black ink from a squid's body that could spew out at any moment and drench someone in gore.

He couldn't erase the terrifying scene from his memory: the girl's face falling apart under the scissors in Jennifer's hand.

He had eventually thrown away the scissors—they looked quite sinister in the form of a crime tool, and he did not want it to belong to his room of happiness.

The first time Mom had met Jennifer, she had informed Charlie how she had felt uncomfortable around her.

Mom always seemed to have a third eye, being able to somewhat foresee the future. Her premonitions, however, never went wrong.

Years ago, while standing at the intersection of the small town in Louisiana where she was born, Mom had spotted the figure of young Dad emerging on the horizon.

He had approached her, asking for directions in an English accent. He had a thin figure but a pair of bright and intelligent eyes and was apparently unfamiliar with the area.

Somehow, she had known at that moment that he would stay back in this dusty, backward town that still drew water from wells and refrigerated food with ice.

She knew he would belong to her, and that he would change her life.

The timer went off, breaking off Charlie's train of thoughts, indicating the completion of the fixing step. Charlie dipped a few sheets of print paper into a large tray of water with a clip and turned on the light.

His eyes fell on the top photo.

Facing the camera, a seven or eight-year-old boy was sitting on the sand beach at the edge of the rising tide. His legs were splayed out together in front of him and his hands laid on his sides, his face holding a reserved smile.

A hundred meters behind him, a man was standing with his legs submerged in the ocean water with his back to the camera, twisting his body like a crooked stake.

It was half an hour before the dolphins appeared.

After rinsing, Charlie carefully picked up the prints and transferred them into the final tray one by one.

It contained a special chemical solution that could detect extremely weak electromagnetic radiation captured in the photos—background electromagnetic radiation from the revolving earth, or almost any living creature present in the surrounding.

It was his secret discovery two years ago. A strange black crystalline carbon salt from the Louisiana swamp was capable of absorbing the weak electromagnetic radiation buried in an exposed photo paper, transforming its molecular structure, and releasing the energy to form an image on the print paper.

He called it *ghost carbon*.

He watched the print intently.

Slowly as the clock ticked, rippling curves emerged circle after circle on the print before him, countless and endless circles with ups and downs like the movement of a symphony. The astonishing curves were emanating and radiating from the ocean as well as from the bodies of the boy and man. They were diffusing and eventually overlapping, as if two musical notebooks had been merged together chemically.

They were the waveforms that he knew so well from his previous encounters with ghost carbon. But never had he seen such extensive radiation in any print.

He pressed the photo paper back into the water tank to rinse it again.

Then he picked up the next photo and repeated the same process until the last one.

When he laid his eyes on the last photo, he was stunned and could hardly believe what he saw.

The original waveforms were all messed up as if being blown off by a sudden and violent hurricane from the sky. The circular forms had been flattened to the horizon.

It was as if the symphony that had been cheerfully playing came to an abrupt end and stopped on a spooky note.

That was the last one before the dolphins appeared. Five minutes earlier.

How could this be possible?

He frowned slightly. Picking it up with a clip, he brought it closer to his face, and examined it carefully.

A12

"Charlie?" Bill's voice sounded confused on the phone.

"Yes, it's me. Remember what I told you about the dolphins a couple of days ago?"

Charlie's voice grew solemn. "I saw what happened. I mean, the incident that had grounded the dolphins on the beach. I saw why it happened."

"You *saw* it?" Bill was puzzled.

"Yes. Remember ghost carbon? Remember how it can absorb weak electromagnetic energy and develop it on photo paper?"

"Of course, I remember."

"I just faxed you. Take a look."

Bill's footsteps sounded, walking away from the phone. He soon returned to the mouthpiece.

"I developed a photo of Miami Beach on ghost carbon-coated paper, taken minutes before the dolphins flocked to the beach. Did you see it? All the electromagnetic signals seemed to tumble down by what looked like a hurricane from the sky," Charlie continued.

"*Oh my God*! Could it really be a radioactive storm from space?!" Bill exclaimed, staring at the faxed photo in his hand.

"That's what I thought. It is the only way that the navigation by the dolphin's magnetic crystals you were talking about, would be messed up, wouldn't it?" Charlie asked.

"That's right. Dolphins and whales migrate long distances across the ocean every year and the Earth's magnetic field is the only map that they can rely on for precision navigation. But the magnetic field is quite vulnerable to solar storms, which can cause these kinds of situations."

"I want to look up data on the timing of past solar magnetic storms and reports of dolphins being stranded on beaches and see how the two correlate." said Charlie.

"Makes sense. Oh wait, I can help with it. I can set it up as a research project for one of my students at the University of Miami."

"That would be great."

"Do you know how close dolphins are to humans?" Bill suddenly changed the subject. "Have you heard the story about the dolphin Pete?"

"Pete?" Questioned Charlie.

"Ten years ago, a bottlenose dolphin named Pete fell in love with Margaret, who had been with him for several weeks for scientific experiments. Her task was to play, sleep, and bathe with him; basically, train him and teach him English.

He liked to touch her with his body—her knees, her feet, her hands.

She didn't feel uncomfortable, so she just let him do it.

But being a woman, she could sense his sexual needs, and when he became insatiable, she arranged for him to be transported away to spend the day with female dolphins. But his desires grew more and more frequent, and it became quite difficult to send him away every time.

To keep him focused on training, Margaret simply comforted him with her hands.

This seemed to save a lot of trouble. She simply tickled him, finished him off quickly, and started her class. For him, however, it was an erotic experience, his romantic relationship with her.

He was there and knew she was there too.

He longed to be with her, and he wouldn't be happy when she wasn't near him.

Shortly after the project was interrupted due to lack of funds, Pete was separated from Margaret and sent to the Dolphin Pool in Florida.

During the weeks there, he insisted on sinking to the bottom of the pool, refusing to breathe, and eventually committed suicide.

Margaret said he was no longer a dolphin.

He was *Pete*."

"What made you bring this up? Sounds like a crazy love story." Charlie laughed.

"Nothing, just thought of it. Thought it was interesting." Bill answered.

A13

Margaret satisfied Pete's desire. Pete fell in love with Margaret. *Pete died for his love.*

Suddenly, the thought of Jennifer approached Charlie, and an indescribable pain filled his chest.

His life was like a mango, chopped into tiny pieces by Jennifer, spread and decorated on a plate, and slowly plopped into her mouth. Yes, it was the pain of being slowly digested, of eroding away in infinity.

Thoughts of Mom, now left alone by the demise of his dad, pulled him back from the lull of infinity. He decided to visit his mother and help her arrange for someone to take care of the pine trees in her backyard.

Mom was sixty-six with high blood pressure and joint aches, despite which she moved around pretty well. She put on a long floral dress and had her hair nicely permed to greet her son. When he walked into the house, her eyes brightened immediately.

After Dad passed away, Mom refused to move away from the old house. She didn't seem to notice that the house was deteriorating. It was the only place where she could cherish her husband's memories. It took Charlie considerable effort to convince her to even replace the roof.

The furniture was still the same, including the old-fashioned silver leather couch in the living room where Dad used to lounge, reading newspapers, watching TV, or occasionally dozing off.

Next to Dad's couch was Mom's chair. Beside her chair stood an end table holding their favorite antique lamp.

Mom and Dad had been together, living in that house for *more than forty years.*

Soft sunlight from the drawing room windows shone on the neat but outdated furniture. There was an indescribable sentiment wafting through the house, making Charlie feel loved and whole again.

It was warm, out of trend, with an air of melancholy hidden in the clumsiness. It preserved all the moments when Mom and Dad were still together as if time had stopped its flow since then.

It was a shell that they had built for themselves, a stubborn hard shell that refused to be eroded by the passing of time or death. In that way, they lived on, *together forever.*

They lived through all the elements in the house, preserving their touch and presence. Even Dad's couch, still occupying the center space in front of the TV, felt as if he could be there any moment, turning his head to talk to Mom about his shop and business.

Charlie used to think that the furniture in the house was boring, ugly, ridiculous, and undisputedly embarrassing. But he slowly understood that it wasn't about the furniture itself, but rather what it reminded of.

Over the years, the lives of Dad and Mom had gradually precipitated into these objects. They had picked up their life, their breaths, their memories, grown together with him and her, and were no longer separable.

They were no longer just simple inanimate objects.

Charlie followed Mom into her bedroom to find piles of woolen yarn of various colors scattered on the bed.

"I'm going to make you a woolen blanket this year. Choose your colors."

Charlie took a quick look and picked up one ball of dark red yarn and another of gray. "Make one out of these", he said.

He couldn't bring himself to say that he had no interest in woolen fabrics.

"Why go to the trouble of weaving a blanket? Just buy something already made." He still couldn't help muttering.

Mom was as hardworking and frugal now as she used to be in the early days in spite of the enormous family wealth.

"It's not the same," she said softly. "The blanket I make will be your company when I'm gone."

Her words touched Charlie's heart.

Mom was the only child of her parents and Charlie was her only child.

Her father surnamed Hoffman, came from Germany alone in his early years. Her mother's family name was Paintings.

After three generations the Paintings had flourished into a family of more than thirty members and were scattered all over Louisiana.

She and Charlie were the only ones from her side. But she remained close to the relatives from the Paintings' side, especially Aunt Emma.

Since childhood, Charlie had seen Mom go to the farm with her helper to pick up fresh beef and red beans, which would be neatly packaged and stored in the huge refrigerator and freezer at home. It was a part of Mom's routine, but she also liked going out onto the field.

In fact, she could cook only a few dishes herself, with sausages and red beans with rice being her specialty.

As afternoon approached, Charlie was held back by Mom for lunch. He sat on the balcony facing the pine forest in the backyard, reviving his childhood, and enjoying her delicious dish with the rich meaty aroma of the sausage mixed in with well-stewed red beans over white rice.

"How's Jennifer?" She hesitated but asked suddenly. Jennifer rarely came to see her.

"Um. Fine. Same, I guess."

Mom never felt well around Jennifer. If Charlie was not the one to introduce her to Mom, she might have very well hated Jennifer. Whenever Jennifer was around, Mom would quiet down. She would change from her usual self, dominated by the overpowering aura of

Jennifer, and quietly go about doing her chores. A slight sneer appeared on Mom's face, and she continued.

"If it's the right person, you would know it, cuz you would really get along. There would be no drama."

Charlie didn't respond right away. He didn't like Mom meddling in his personal life, but in this aspect he was bound to agree with her.

"Mom don't worry about it. I know what to do." He ended the topic quietly.

Mom stopped, trying hard to hide her worries.

She changed the topic and began chatting about what was going on in Aunt Emma's house. Her eyes glowed when she informed him that Aunt Emma's daughter, Catherine, was planning a family reunion early next year.

Honestly, Charlie wasn't interested. He never understood people's obsession with blood ties or genetic succession. Blood would have been so diluted and mixed beyond recognition through generations of genetic recombination.

He didn't want to be held hostage by blood.

It was a meaningless mission.

Like God, it was a falsehood created by the mankind himself.

Neither wanting to hurt Mom nor be a part of the genetic mess, he apologized to Mom, saying he had a plan with friends to rent a house and ski in Colorado early next year after the holidays.

Mom sighed but said nothing.

She got up and went to the kitchen. She had ordered dessert from Charlie's favorite old, local cake shop.

"Mom, you really don't know anything about Dad's past?" Charlie was eating the banana split when he asked curiously.

"Except for the fact that he was from England, no one knew anything about him. He literarily appeared out of thin air, wearing a wrinkled suit, a round hat, and a pair of dusty brown leather shoes, like a beleaguered noble.

Everyone called him *Ed from England.*

I did ask him, early on and later during our lives. He said nothing. He took his secret to the grave.

He was well-educated, extremely knowledgeable, and intelligent, unlike the locals. It was a chaotic time. Even if he was a wanted gangster or criminal, who would care? Why provoke something which does not disturb us?"

Mom smiled, her eyes glowing softly as if Dad was standing right in front of her.

"Charlie, how are your investments?" Mom asked, looking a bit concerned.

"Still with Bear Sterns in New York. I talked to Ace on the phone the other day. He just divorced Ann. He's already making money on the companies he'd scooped up when the market crashed.

This guy's so sharp. There's no money that he can't make. Completely different from Dad. Dad worked hard for every penny. Rumor has it that Ace is in line to be the next CEO of Bear Sterns."

"Watch out for the risks, Charlie. Easy money can also be lost quickly." Mom cautioned him.

A14

September 10, 1976. Louisiana.

Early morning.

Following his morning routine, Charlie was finishing up his jog in the pine forest in the Zemmuray Garden.

The forest was infused with the fresh scent of pines. Occasionally, the morning breeze whispered through and blew off some pine needles.

Sunlight filtered through rows of trees, casting a shadowy canopy on the ground.

It was early autumn, but he soon felt the increasingly sultry heat.

The weather forecast had entitled the day to be a sweltering day, with the highs in the 90s.

Feeling a little suffocated and parched, Charlie decided to end the run early.

After a good shower, he came down straight to the large dining room.

A platter of morning newspapers consisting of the New York Times, Washington Post, New Orleans tabloid, and The Times-Picayune, were already fanned on the dining table, along with coffee and breakfast by Mr. Montgomery, who had picked them up from the front gate.

Charlie now sat down, sipping his coffee.

He flipped through the New York Times and paused on page sixteen.

Right in the center of the page was an unfamiliar photograph of Tiananmen Square in Beijing, China.

The flag was half lowered and rows of Chinese people, plainly dressed, were standing in mourning, with their backs facing the camera.

Next to it was Beijing's official announcement of the death of the Chairman Mao.

A few short commentaries followed the announcement: *Mao Zedong, the leader of China's Red Revolution, died in Beijing at the age of 82.*

It was a rare piece of news about China, which did not interest Charlie at first.

China was simply an abstract existence marked somewhere on the map.

It was far away, unfamiliar, and irrelevant to him.

His eyes almost automatically moved on from the page, but somehow his hand stopped, forcing him to look at the page opened in front of him.

Beyond all the crowd and all the newspaper articles, the image of Yinyi floated in front of his eyes. He could see *her.* He could see *her* there!

Behind the visuals.

Behind his consciousness.

The irrelevant China suddenly became a secret crossway that was inevitably tangled with his fate.

His heart fluttered, overwhelmed with tenderness.

He carefully examined the photo.

He had seen China in 1989, caught drastically in a political storm.

He had met Yinyi there.

The thought almost choked him with its intensity. The thought that he had deliberately avoided.

He kept forcing himself not to think about it, but it kept dragging him into a secret excitement and anxiety.

It was as if he had stumbled upon a door leading to a secret passage. He had accidentally pushed the door open and took a causal glance into the passage and now he could no longer shut the door close and walk away like nothing had happened.

It was secretly waiting for him to return.

It had successfully cast its spell on him.

He could clearly remember his heartbeat when Yinyi had appeared in front of his eyes.

He could still feel the warmth of the faint sunlight filtering through the windows, when she was cleaning his wounds, shy and focused.

But now, in 1976, she should just be a 9-year-old girl in China that had long been shut closed to the world.

Neither her time nor her place had anything to do with him.

But there had been something between the two of them, in 1989, or before.

What was it?!

What was the secret between them, unknown to him, hidden in their past or future?

He *did not* know.

He *wanted* to know.

A15

Mr. Montgomery, clutching onto the mails of the day, hurried to the game house behind the main building.

The game house was a secret hideout of Charlie, adorned with bookshelves, a fireplace and sofa chairs on one end, and a large rectangular marble platform with various scientific instruments and tools on the other. On a wall-sized whiteboard hung Charlie's design sketches and drawings, adding to the mystery of the room.

It was a replica of the backyard guest house in Charlie's childhood home, but fancier and more complex, with all sorts of cutting-edge tools and equipment. The setup was completed with a silver pipe protruding from the ceiling, leading to a huge opening hanging over the entire marble workbench to vent any harmful gas.

It was here that he extracted the ghost carbon from the swamp mud.

It was an extremely accidental discovery. Charlie and his friends were paddling in the swamp at the southern end of the local Lake Pontchartrain, and he was busy taking pictures of the moss-covered cypress trees with great interest, when accidentally he dropped his photo paper package into the swamp.

It was a totally unexpected phenomenon as if guided by fate. He hired someone to salvage the package of his favorite photographic paper from the bottom of the lake. When he went on to use them later for his new photos, he found an unusual darker tint on the photo papers. Knowing that the package had remained intact the entire while, his scientific mind kicked in and he instantly thought of some kind of gas that might have permeated into the papers from the swamp. He was shocked to find electromagnetic fields revealed in the photos, which he later was able to attribute to the layer of the strange coating deposited on the photographic paper.

Out of excitement, Charlie soon dug up the mud from the same spot and transported it to his garden.

He spent days and nights researching and experimenting, filtering out rocks, isolating out gases, and was eventually able to condense them and extract a new carbon material that looked like black silk.

He named it *Ghost Carbon*.

The first person that he called after his discovery was Bill. Bill got so excited that he proposed drafting an article and publishing it in a top academic journal like Nature or Science. He was certain that Charlie was going to be famous.

But Charlie had just frowned slightly and replied that he was simply not interested.

Instead, he hired a local craftsman and made a lone wolf out of the ghost carbon and displayed it on his workbench.

Charlie was sitting in his beloved game house with his feet up on the table, staring at the ghost carbon lone wolf seated on a cherry wood frame, when he heard footsteps behind him.

Mr. Montgomery had entered the room, with an unusual look on his face, his hands full of mail. His face portrayed a conflicting array of emotions, with vague excitement mixed with deep regret and sadness that he was struggling to conceal.

Charlie noticed it and couldn't help but wonder.

"Mr. Montgomery, is everything okay?"

"All good. Charlie..."

"Mmm?"

"Miss Gill is getting married. This is her wedding invitation." Mr. Montgomery revealed a golden envelope in his hand.

"Oh." Charlie acknowledged it without enthusiasm or display of any emotions and took the envelope.

Miss *Gill Charlotte* used to be Charlie's classmate at Yale and belonged to a prominent family. She was beautiful, outgoing, and crazy about Charlie. Charlie and Charlotte had been engaged once.

A picture-perfect young couple with well-matched family backgrounds; they were blessed by everyone from both sides. Their engagement was announced in the newspapers in a high profile.

Unfortunately, things started turning down when Charlie's father unexpectedly passed away. Charlie's school was also interrupted as he joined the army to go to South Korea where his first stop was El Paso Fort Bliss by the Mexican border.

One morning, following a full night of brutal military training, Charlie rushed back from the shower, exhausted, to pick up a call from Gill in the noisy and chaotic barracks of Fort Bliss.

He clutched the phone tightly but could barely hear her. Her voice was faint, drifting away, and became even fainter, as if she was struggling to breathe, struggling to escape from him.

She informed Charlie that she was on a vacation in Saint Tropez, France, with a real estate man. They had just stopped in front of a hotel and the man had gone inside to check in.

She said she was alone watching the colorful reflection of the streetlights on the other side of a canal, that the night wind was a little chilly, and that she was pregnant with the man's child.

She apologized for what she had done and said that she would be tortured by the guilt for Charlie for the rest of her life.

But it had been really hard for her to be left alone for so long and that she had been really lonely.

The moment he put down the phone, Charlie was no longer aware of what he saw or heard.

The surroundings suddenly emptied and quieted down.

It was as if he wasn't standing in the noisy and chaotic Quonset hut with a heavy traffic of imprudent young soldiers, but rather he was standing all alone on a deserted shore, facing a boundless ocean under the gray sky.

And the sky was collapsing right in front of him.

The ocean quickly receded, exposing the rising and falling profile of the rocky ancient floor.

He was left there at a loss, standing alone at the edge of life.

His body lost all its warmth and turned into a heavy stone pillar, or a giant statue on the Easter Island, beaten down by wind and rain. He started to sink into the sand under his feet.

He kept sinking and was being buried over.

It felt like a sudden death, a death that allowed no time for sorrow, as if his soul was lost, taken away by the frigid wind.

It kept drifting in the air, with no destination, until it slowly, thoroughly disintegrated.

Standing in a trance, he was vaguely aware that someone approached him, patted him on the shoulder, smiled, and mumbled something.

By instinct, he landed his eyes on the face, but he was too blind to see. He forced a smile in response, nodded, and walked away.

That was the last time he had spoken to her.

He didn't mention it to anyone. Instead, he downplayed it, simply saying that it was a mutual decision since both of them had drifted apart as a result of their separation.

Next, when he heard of Gill was when she had given birth to a girl out of wedlock. He found it weird how he had completely let go of the past. It even creeped him out to think that he had been so close to being fooled into a vulgar marriage and he felt fortunate it had not happened.

Nonetheless, he sent her a simple ceremonial blessing.

By the time he met Jennifer, he had lost his slightest interest in marriage.

Charlie sat, reading the wedding invitation. Next to Gill's name was an unfamiliar Italian man's name.

"Charlie, did you get a call from Jennifer?" Mr. Montgomery asked with a bit of hesitation, still standing in front of Charlie.

"Nope."

"She called every day when you weren't home. Sometimes, several times a day. She sounded really upset." Mr. Montgomery said as gently as possible.

"Oh."

"Can you call her?'

"Okay, I will. Thank you, Mr. Montgomery."

A16

Charlie briefly reflected on it. Although reluctant to acknowledge it, he realized that in the center of the mess, he was surprisingly burdened by his guilt for Jennifer: guilt for the fact that he denied her wish to get married and raise a family.

He eventually dialed her number.

But the phone was only screaming in vain. No one answered.

In the afternoon, he drove to a store to pick up a couple of electronic parts.

The air was still hot, but the sky unexpectedly darkened. By the time Charlie had reached the store, a light shower had started, and it took no time for the streets and trees to be engulfed by the misty rain.

He stepped out of the store and ran to his car, deciding that he might very well just sit in the car and watch the white streetlamps and hanging flower baskets immersed in the drizzle.

Suddenly, Charlie heard a knock on the window.

He turned his head and saw the face of a young girl; a large bouquet in her arms, eagerly asking him if he wanted some flowers.

He immediately nodded, rolled down the window, took the flowers, and handed over the cash.

She thanked him happily and ran away back into the rain.

The rich fragrance of the fresh flowers diffused in the car—Dahlia, purple chrysanthemum, and veronica spicata.

All those symbolizing beauty and love in the world of humankind.

Charlie was infected by the joy from the flowers and the girl and had the sudden urge to put aside his worries and embrace happiness.

He started the car and headed straight to Jennifer's house.

As usual, he parked his car on the driveway.

But as he turned around, he caught a glimpse of an unfamiliar red Audi on the side of the road.

The more he stared at it, an ominous premonition crept into his subconscious.

The rain turned into a drizzle now with a shroud of mist hanging in the distance.

He hesitated for a moment but instinctively rejected the hunch.

He had never looked forward to happiness so enthusiastically. He was already fantasizing about the fresh happiness blooming between him and Jennifer.

Just like what she had promised him time and time again.

He persuaded himself into holding the flowers and walking through the drizzle to the door.

He rang the doorbell and waited.

As if guided by fate in the dark, he had arrived uninvited on that rainy day, not earlier or later, and reached out to ring the doorbell at that particular time.

When the door opened, the darkness finally blinded him, and he immediately understood that everything between him and Jennifer was completely over.

Jennifer stood in the doorway, surprised and embarrassed, with a man who had stepped forward to wrap his arms around her waist.

Charlie recognized him. It was the pilot who had flirted with her in the bar.

The flowers dropped from Charlie's hands, and he turned and walked away without a word.

A17

In the following months, Charlie seemed to have disappeared completely from the public eye.

Various concert tours and bars had opened all over the city.

The endless partying brought people together on the streets of Louisiana.

Parades and carnivals flooded the streets of New Orleans.

Every young body swayed in the pleasure of indulgence. Every old soul remained intoxicated by the timeless music from the past.

The passionate performers, struggling in the crowd, were always found on the streets or in the alleys of the French Quarter, plucking onto melancholy blues and turning sadness into utter bliss.

Everyone was swept up into a whirlpool of happiness, fun, and melody.

The joy of physical indulgence, the joy of being amidst the cheer of the crowd, the joy of drinking and having crawfish.

The joy of watching the bright and shiny Mardi Gras beads being thrown out into the air.

The joy of stepping on the confetti on the ground.

The joy of making love.

It was nothing but utter exuberance, with no allowance for conscious thinking or fear.

No one paused to notice the broken souls and the worn-out bodies that the passing time had chipped away, like a brick wall that was slowly eroding, with its colors gradually mottled, or like the hands of an old alarm clock that had quietly rusted and slowed down.

Louisiana had turned into a caravan of jubilance, a caravan stagnating in the sea of exhilaration.

That year, the Vietnam War came to an end.

Jimmy Carter became the 39th President of the United States and Star Wars hit the theaters.

Charlie quietly vanished from this vigorous social caravan. Once a familiar social figure, he now took his leave from the path of joy.

He declined all the invitations to parties or social events, and kept himself at the Zemmuray Garden, busy sifting through a large pile of materials on time and space.

The only time he went out was to get copies of books or journals from the libraries.

The theory about the *"closed timeline curves"* in the Gödel formula for space–time particularly attracted his attention. Bill had mentioned it to him the last time they met.

Time was no longer a one-way straight line, but a closed curve. There was no beginning or end, and therefore no precedence.

Einstein had also mentioned in the "*Philosophers, Scientists*" that one should abandon the physical description of the sequence of events.

The more Charlie read, the more he believed that these curves were organically overlapping and intersecting, to construct a complex and wonderful space-time existence.

The fantasies from their youth became even more irresistible now, although there was no way to verify.

The only hints peeking at the truth of their fantasies were those bizarre natural phenomena that could not be explained by any existing theory.

Just like *the begonia flower* he had brought back from the Bermuda Triangle.

The memory of the flower instantaneously drew him back to that day when he was drifting into the deep ocean of the Caribbean, diving into its depths.

The sunlight was blocked out by the heavy water above and only the translucent weak rays floating in from the sun revealed the ocean floor.

Multiple shadows were floating in the water, the shadows of his swinging limbs.

The shadows of gigantic seaweeds.

The shadows of fish swimming by in schools, silently.

The shadows of the clouds in the sky.

Then, it came to him—that extraordinary bubble that took him to 1989's China, to Yinyi.

The bubble was an amalgamation of the past, present and future—blown up by a strong wind of a secret swelling energy. It grew bigger and bigger, and finally engulfed the scattered wormholes, bridging the interfaces of the lurking exotic matter of space and time.

Charlie saw those floating shadows on the bubble, those soft shadows, emerging from the multitude of times—the shadows of a series of events, the shadows of fragments of long films running on this planet.

Those individual segments were playing out at the same time, with neither beginning nor end.

All those shadows were drifting in and out of the wormholes, sometimes overlapping, sometimes scattered, sometimes bright, and sometimes dim.

Like the colors of a rainbow, the shadows merged into each other, hidden in the wormholes, rendering him unable to identify them; the wormholes with only curved surfaces that carried no borders or corners.

Swallowed by the radiant bubble, he was immediately drowned in the darkness of the innumerable space-time dimensions.

Exotic matter. Exotic matter with extreme negative energy.

He recalled the strange conversions within the properties of the water at that moment and how his body had shrunk and dissolved.

He was convinced that his body was being engulfed by an abnormal energy, an anomalous source of mysterious, powerful energy.

Charlie turned out the map, his fingers roaming around, pointing, until he reached the place where he drew a circle with a crayon to mark the sea area of *the Devil's Triangle*.

He stared at it, thinking about the dolphins stranded in Miami and Bill's promise of information on historic solar magnetic storm activities.

It was time for him to see Bill.

A18

An upcoming trip to New York took Charlie to the Bear Sterns investment firm.

There was news that the Indian textile giant, Reliance, was preparing to go public in November and Bear Sterns intended to discuss investment matters with Charlie.

Charlie wasn't into the hustle and bustle of New York City. The rush and speed neither appealed nor attracted him.

After the meeting and the signing of papers, he walked out of the Bear Stern Building at 333 Madison Avenue in Manhattan. He looked up only to see a gloomy heaven blocked and cut by the skyscrapers, and depression descended on him again.

The crowd on the street was rushing in all directions, with emotionless faces and an air of complete indifference, in an obvious effort to steer clear of each other's path.

It seemed to him that people, just like the particles of matter, could only survive at a proper distance from each other. If they got too close, they would hate and repel each other, leading to their own destruction.

Ace laughed when he heard Charlie's thoughts and commented that Charlie was a spoilt Louisiana rich man with his own garden.

"Do you know why so many people live in New York?" Ace questioned knowingly.

"Because human instinct is to cuddle together to stay warm.

Humans belong in a herd. They are social animals.

But you are not.

You are *a lone wolf*, although being way more capable than anyone else to command the attention of every living soul."

Charlie planned to fly to Florida before returning to New Orleans. He needed to pay Bill a visit.

He arrived at New York's JFK airport just on time and checked into the lounge. Grabbing a coffee and a piece of blueberry cake, he sat down in a corner against a glass wall, glancing out of the window.

A thin ray of sunlight had burst out between the heavy clouds, casting a translucent shroud over the airport. It could easily be mistaken as a cool khaki color moonlight pouring down over the airport.

The yellowish hues of the sun were soft, dark, and silent, as if countless fine and obscure smoke particles were gliding in the air and slowly settling on everything, transforming the entire world into a faded old photograph.

Little did he know that this old photo would forever be framed in his memory because of what would follow ten minutes later.

It was 6:30 in the evening.

Charlie had just checked his wristwatch when a blaring announcement called his name repeatedly from the nearby speakers.

He would never forget that moment.

He heard his name echoing in the airport lounge. Without any hunch, he stood up and walked to the reception in the VIP lounge.

The well-trained female staff member handed over the phone with an odd look, informing that an emergency call was waiting for him.

He picked up the phone. It was Aunt Emma.

As soon as he heard her voice, his heart struck down. The premonition of a bad feeling bore down upon him.

Aunt Emma rarely contacted him directly. She usually hung out with Mom.

Something must have happened for her to feel the urgency to talk to him when he was still traveling.

He felt an inexplicable panic rising in his stomach, his breathing hitched, and his fingers curled tightly around the telephone receiver.

However, he forced himself to calm down.

"Charlie…" Aunt Emma's voice sounded unusually grave.

"I'm here." Charlie answered.

But Aunt Emma seemed at a loss for words. On the phone, Charlie could vaguely hear the choked crying she was trying to restrain.

Then he heard her. Speaking with extreme difficulty, her voice sounded slow and dim.

"Your mom had a heart attack today when we went out for a haircut together.

I took her to the emergency room.

But she didn't make it to the hospital.

Charlie…

She passed away an hour ago.

I've been looking for you since then. You need to come back, Charlie."

She couldn't bear it any longer and burst into tears, holding onto the phone.

Standing there, Charlie felt something he had never felt before.

He suddenly felt cold and stiff all over his body, his consciousness frozen into unconscious icicles. He tried to hang on, like the icicles hanging from the edge of the roofs, waiting to collapse and shatter at the slightest touch.

His eye sockets became two volcanic wells, exposed to the air in his whole frozen body. Warm tears gurgled out of their own accord, breaking his soul like scattered icicles, pouring down, freezing his entire existence.

He stood still like a statue carved into stone. So silently, tears rolled down his cheeks, as he clutched onto the phone numbly like holding on to the ultimate straw.

He could no longer hear Aunt Emma's voice.

Enormous emptiness engulfed him. Everything was lost, all at once. Desolation and loneliness gradually descended on him.

He became extremely fragile, like a baby that needed compassion from everyone.

His heart was wrenched out from his chest, leaving a big hollow hole. He looked down, feeling lost and isolated.

The overwhelming grief turned his blood into an icy stream.

The loss flowed down, tearing and cutting from head to toe.

It was the end of the world. His world.

As his mother trespassed the realm of death, something in Charlie left with her too. A part of him died with her that day.

On the other side of the border between life and death, he stared blankly at his broken self.

Mechanically, he changed his ticket and rushed home.

On his arrival, Aunt Emma related his mom's last words to him: "Charlie's busy. I won't see him anymore."

Although the funeral was a bit rushed and low-key as intended, it was a decent ceremony, thanks to Mr. Montgomery.

Mr. Montgomery revealed to Charlie that the year Charlie's dad died, his mom had secretly arranged for her own funeral. The funeral home, the burial site, the approximate number of guests, as such, were all spelled out in her plan. She had even put aside a budget to cover the expense.

Charlie suddenly understood why he had always felt that his parents had never parted from each other.

For Mom, Dad was always there, had always been with her, and on another journey in the underworld, was still waiting for her.

After the funeral, everyone including Mr. Montgomery was gone and Charlie was left alone in his mom's house.

The house was eerily quiet, quieter than quiet as if it had sunk into a meditation of mystical memories.

He could almost hear the quiet churning of the air stirred up by his walk, or the gentle fall of the soft sunlight filtered in from the windows on the floor.

Voices filled up Charlie's ears, lots of voices, from the living room, the kitchen, the hallway, the bedroom, they came from every corner.

Voices arrived from the outdated sofa, the coffee table, the lamp, the ceiling fans; everything seemed to be breathing, everything seemed to be alive.

Voices that were buried in time were unable to leave.

He could hear the cacophony of news on the TV, even when it was off, or the voices of his mom casually chatting with his dad.

Their voices were on and off; far and near.

They were simple chitchats that revealed little of their emotions. But as soon as one spoke, the other would immediately follow, like two seemingly careless birds always twittering back faithfully to each other.

Those voices were now hidden in this empty old house as if it was a message bottle drifting in the ocean of time.

The message bottle that was noticed by nobody except Charlie.

Charlie stepped into his parents' bedroom.

As he went inside the walk-in closet, he spotted a new blanket. It was neatly folded and kept in a plastic bag, as if ready to be transferred.

A hand-made blanket in dark red and grey.

His heart started to pound, his eyes burned and blurred. He picked up the bag, rushed back to the bedroom, and slowly spread the blanket on the bed.

It was completely finished.

He reached out and touched it gently. A warm and densely knitted woolen blanket.

He heard his mom's voice again.

"It can be your company when I'm gone."

Her voice rang in his ears as Charlie held on to the blanket close to his heart. His shoulders started to tremble. He could no longer hold back his tears.

He realized that from now on, he would be an orphan.

A19

There were always moments like this when Bill stood by Charlie's side, despite the fact that Elizabeth had just given birth a few days ago.

When Charlie walked out of his mom's house, he saw Bill sitting in a wicker chair on the front porch.

They hadn't seen each other for a long time. Bill had transformed from an inexperienced young man into a gentle and charming scholar.

Bill stood up as Charlie approached.

No words passed between them. They hugged and held each other.

"I'm so sorry. I'm late." Bill said.

"That's ok. How are Liz and the baby?" Charlie asked.

"All good. Mother and baby are both doing well."

"Great. Congratulations again."

"Thanks." Bill replied. He paused for a moment, and said, "Charlie, we named her Lilian."

Charlie's eyes misted up.

Lillian was Charlie's mother's name.

Bill stayed back with Charlie that night in his garden, and they talked through the whole night. They recollected the memories of their childhood spent in Charlie's house and the memories of Charlie's mom came up inevitably.

Bill recalled how Charlie's mom treated him many times at her house and the story of her blueberry pie.

He remembered vividly many of the details: how Charlie's mom quietly offered him food and clothes after he had caught cold running with Charlie in the rain, how she made him hot chicken soup; and when he and Charlie got into trouble, how she came forward to settle everything.

To Bill, they were the warmest and most beautiful memories of his humble childhood, and to him, Charlie's parents were the kindest and most generous people in the world.

Charlie was amazed at Bill's memory. All the stories sounded familiar to him, but they were rather fuzzy and fragmented instead of precisely detailed as in Bill's remembrance.

He had never thought much about his mom's kindness, and it wasn't until now that he realized how lucky he was to have a mother like her.

Loss and grief still overpowered him, but slowly he felt something awakening in his body. It was something that had been seeded and secretly nurtured over time under the care of his mother.

It was a warm power from the deepest part of his soul, a spiritual power that death could not vanquish.

It was the fundamental and unwavering love for life and living beings.

It was the unending kindness of his mother that had been embedded in him.

It was the fire seeded in his body by her. At this moment, when he was lonely in the dark, it burst into flames, rose up, and illuminated him.

Charlie's thoughts drifted towards his recent discoveries about the Bermuda Triangle, and he shared with Bill his latest reflections.

He talked about the Van Ellen Belt and the South Atlantic Anomaly, known as *the Bermuda Triangle in space*. He said that the Earth was wearing a protective suit of magnetic field to block off the high-energy particles from the sun and the universe, but unfortunately, there was a thin, leaking spot in the suit and it was the South Atlantic Anomaly. There the Earth's magnetic field was exceptionally weak, and the particles of energy radiated by the sun were closest to the Earth, only 120 miles away.

"But the Bermuda Triangle is North of it in the Atlantic." Bill looked unsure.

"That's right. However, there's antimatter for matter. Similarly, there's also possibly anti-energy for energy."

"Yes. It could be an image relationship." Bill nodded.

They were fascinated by the idea. They started picturing the Earth floating in a river in space, the Earth's magnetic field and the radioactive particles measurable and visible, like trees or clouds above the ground. They simultaneously cast symmetrical reflections in the river, the unfathomable anti-energy.

Their ideas flowed like their imagination where countless rivers flowed in time and space, with countless reflections.

Just like a curved surface showing convex and concave images at the same time.

"Getting back to the Bermuda Triangle, to Miami Beach, the preliminary modeling data we found, nay, generated, suggested a positive correlation between the dolphins stranded on the beach and the solar storm activity. We want to collect more data and conduct the strongest statistical analysis for a good paper." Bill confirmed with sparks in his eyes.

"Oh indeed." Charlie smiled. "That means solar storms do affect the energy field of the Bermuda Triangle rather uniquely. In that case, I think I know what I'm going to do."

Bill was confused. "What do you mean? *What are you going to do Charlie?*"

A20

For the next two months, Charlie plunged himself into collecting, researching, analyzing all historical data on solar storms and activities, learning their relative positions and connections to each other. Series of data generated into formulas and calculations on astronomical data were verified and re-verified. He sank into the world of the future, extrapolating his ideas into his world of fantasy. Finally, the day arrived. Charlie nailed down the significant day.

He stood in the game house, staring at the crowded drawings and formulas on the whiteboard.

Clearing up everything, he carefully wrote down a single date on the pristine whiteboard: *November 7, 1978.*

The day that an unusual solar storm would hit the earth.

He circled it and wrote down: *Charlie's Bubble.*

His excitement reached its peak. From now on, his sole task would be to prepare for an unusual journey on this special day.

He had almost a year and a half left.

In the days that followed, he tried to think through every possible scenario on the trip and figure out how he could deal with it and how he should be prepared.

He finally put together a list of action items with a timeline.

He would have to execute the plan carefully and flawlessly.

There would be no room for mistakes or omissions.

It would be a solitary experiment for him, one with no chance to revise or redo.

It could be his death or an elixir for life.

The rest would be what he would leave behind—hundreds of millions of dollars of his family wealth. But that was the simple part.

His lawyers had already drawn up an asset plan for him. He now only needed to assign power of attorney to someone to oversee the disposal of the assets for him.

Of course, it would be Bill.

Bill.

Charlie suddenly realized that there was one last thing that he needed to do. While on his journey, he would have to let Bill track him in real-time so that they could communicate in real-time.

He would have to create something that would be a part of his body and would connect him to Bill on a unique time-traveling channel.

It was an extremely crazy idea.

But not impossible.

Charlie thought of the electrical induction between the twins.

He had always believed in the existence of bio-signals in the body, the kind of signals that only complex biological cells could carry.

He would need these bio-signals to allow a unique channel for him and Bill in that signal range. He needed to first work on channeling the bio-signals with the smallest unit possible, burying it in a biofilm as thin as a cicada's wing, and covertly implanting it in his and Bill's ears. The electromagnetic waves buried in those private signals between him and Bill would then need to be converted into quantum to help them communicate over the dimensions of time and space.

He would need a medium to convert conversations in the form of electromagnetic waves into a combined stream of quantum signals.

A quantum trajectory multiplexer.

He could almost visualize it.

A small pearl-colored box, hidden in an abandoned conch shell and quietly buried deep into the ocean. Against the plain sight of the endless waves of tourists, it would be the thing that secretly connected him and Bill.

A21

October 1, 1978. Sunday. Nassau.

A clear blue sky shone high above, the white clouds floating indecisively amidst.

At the humble Nassau International Airport, a plane from Miami landed and taxied slowly on the ground.

Among the passengers, a familiar face rushed out through the yellow two-story terminal building.

Pulling a black suitcase with him, Charlie stopped at the custom window and handed out his passport.

Behind the window was a chubby Black female officer in the uniform of a white coat and a pair of black trousers. She grabbed his passport and looked at it blankly, bored of her daily routine.

"*Edward Johnson*?" She asked mechanically, glancing at Charlie.

"Yes." Charlie answered.

"Business or vacation?"

"Vacation."

One minute later, the officer threw the passport back.

"Welcome to the Bahamas." She said, almost robotically.

"Thank you."

Charlie continued his walk toward the exit of the building. Shortly he was picked up by a local man.

The man drove Charlie to a long and narrow island in Old Ford Bay. Sitting in the backseat, Charlie took his time, noticing the man driving him to his destination. Even though dressed in an airy floral printed shirt, his physique seemed to be one of his greatest strengths. His dark skin almost mixed with his pitch-black hair, cropped close to his skull.

The road was mostly deserted, uninhabited, and bewildering. At the end of the road, a single-story mansion unexpectedly came into view.

The house was only known to Charlie in pictures he had seen much earlier.

He got out of the car and checked on the tropical palm trees that wrapped around the house. They were dense and lush, hiding the house in its embrace.

He followed the man into the house; the food and daily necessities were already prepared for him inside.

Charlie made his way through the huge white hall with its high white roof and headed straight for the backyard.

The white roof extended into an almost overhanging porch, providing a great shady area in the back. A casual but comfortable white leather sofa, few rattan chairs, and many blooming bougainvillea sat around in the shade.

A few steps further was a crystal-clear swimming pool, and beyond that lay a dock in the bay.

His eyes suddenly lit up. Under the bright sunshine was a panoramic view of the beautiful blue bay.

Looking further along the banks of the bay, he could only vaguely see a few scattered houses.

That's it. If all goes well, I will be spending my last month here. He told himself.

After a while the man leaned in from behind Charlie.

"Mr. Johnson, the five wooden boxes you sent earlier have also been placed here. Would you like to take an inventory?"

"Oh. No need. Thanks."

"Is there anything else you need?"

"That's all for now. If anything else, I will contact you." Charlie said, passing down a roll of bills. "Thank you, Mike."

Michael bowed, thanked him, and left.

Charlie's wooden boxes, all with mailing labels and seals, were piled up in an unused guest bedroom with white shutters. Taking a screwdriver out of his black suitcase, he set about opening the boxes.

As the screws from the boxes came out, dismantled parts of the instrument exposed one after another.

Charlie took them out and carefully placed them on a shockproof marble table next to the wall, another special arrangement he had Mike make.

He took out the last piece, an old and ordinary-looking conch shell. However, this was not a regular shell. It was a replica made of a special polymer material blended with crushed shells and aluminum that could resist heavy pressure without shattering. The tiny conch shell held a minute pearl-colored box, containing his microcircuit boards for the quantum trajectory multiplexer. This would resonate with the magnetic waves between Charlie and Bill, allowing them to communicate even in Charlie's other dimensions.

He had also mixed a little ghost carbon in it. On the inside of the conch shell, a small carbon-colored begonia flower was secretly printed.

Charlie's eyes lingered on the flower, the flower that Yinyi had given him.

A22

Charlie rented himself a car to drive around the island.

He needed to know his surroundings.

Nassau Island was a must-stop for cruise ships in the Caribbean. Brought in by the giant cruise ships, tourists flocked to the island and crowded the famous attractions such as Paradise Island, Cable Beach, and the Pirate Museum.

Charlie had no interest in tourist destinations. He decided to roam around on the streets along the coast, getting a feel of the city and the locals.

It was Prince George Wharf. In the distance, a huge cruise ship was moored and nearby, people crowded in shops and eateries under the extended porches of the colonial buildings.

Summer seemed to have forgotten to leave. As the sun broke the morning fog, the temperature quickly climbed over 90 degrees.

With a full dose of UV rays, the sunlight poured straight down, making blinding splashes on the mirror of the blue Caribbean Sea, scorching every living being on the island.

Everywhere on the streets and alleys were stands selling foods, drinks, straw hats, parasols, or local artifacts.

People just passed through, enjoying the coastal breeze, submerging in their joy and laughter. A few boys and girls could be heard laughing. They decided to follow each other to jump onto the coastal parapet, screaming, and playfully dropping into the water.

The beats of the music rose and faded in the air, setting the mood for dancing and joyful indulgence.

Happiness felt so close like the ocean breeze caressing Charlie's face. It was within his arm's reach. It was everywhere.

But Charlie was too broken, too alone to indulge in this happy picture. His thoughts reminded him that sadly, *there was no one left to attach him to this happy world.*

As he kept walking, Charlie's eyes caught at a low-rise yellow concrete wall standing on the pier.

The walls stretched out into the ocean, closing in around a humble wooden restaurant on the water.

As he gazed more, hunger rumbled in his stomach. He walked straight up to the restaurant.

It was noisy and crowded inside. People were busy drinking, eating, and laughing. A couple of old and clumsy ceiling fans were buzzing, stirring up the salty ocean breeze.

Charlie looked out into the ocean and spotted a white lighthouse.

As soon as Charlie sat down at a wooden table by the ocean, a young couple of hippies came over and asked if they could share the table.

Charlie wanted to say no. He had no desire to get close to anyone. But he was softened by their eager anticipation.

He nodded, and the two immediately sat down happily.

The girl was barely twenty, looking innocent, wearing a bare-shouldered long dress. Her dark golden curly hair spread out like a vine, tied down only around her forehead with a thin strap.

The boy was obviously about the same age, tall and thin, wearing a white long-sleeved shirt and a necklace with a dark blue gem; confidence and pretentious sophistication oozing from his manners.

"I'm Paul and she's Lisa." The boy introduced themselves.

"Edward Johnson", Charlie replied without much enthusiasm.

"We're from California. We're eloping." While waiting for the drink, the boy began confessing to Charlie.

"Our parents never approved of us, but we love each other. We're trying to make some money; looking for something to do here.

Once we have enough money, we will get married, buy a farm somewhere and have a couple of kids."

Paul said and turned his eyes to Lisa with affection.

Lisa, shy and happy, smiled and rested her head on Paul's shoulder.

Charlie wondered why he had let two teenagers share his table. Paul and Lisa were so engrossed in their young love that they kept raving about their own stories with no intention of questioning Charlie. Not that it troubled him, but he was least interested in knowing someone else's story.

It wasn't until Lisa got up for the bathroom that Paul pulled out some cash from his pocket and started to count in frustration.

"Not much money left. I need to save money to buy Lisa a ring," he murmured. "I don't want Lisa to worry about it. I kept telling her we are fine."

Charlie was in disbelief. The boy had nothing but a dream of love. He was doomed.

Charlie felt a sudden pity for him.

"Where are you staying?" Charlie asked.

"A hippie friend's house. You know, a shelter for the homeless."

"Give me your address." Charlie said.

Paul froze for a moment, then looked up at Charlie, scared and puzzled.

"If you don't mind, I'd like to keep in touch." Charlie smiled.

"Oh. Certainly. Mr. Johnson, it would be great to see you again." Paul said and quickly wrote his name and contact on a piece of napkin.

Having a hearty meal of fresh seafood, Charlie was back on the secluded Love Beach.

He recognized the white house shaded by the trees on the left and the low wall with countless shells on the right.

He walked over the white sandy beach in the front, which gradually immersed into the Caribbean Sea.

Countless light spots and shadows danced in the shallow, crystal-clear waters.

A light greenish blue hue tinted the initial waters, then the blue deepened layer by layer, and finally turned into a dreamlike dark blue in the distance.

It reminded Charlie of the dark blue in Van Gogh's starry night, the dark blue only possible with concentrated paints, the dark blue that would set a soul free of the body and the world.

He walked over to the ocean.

Gazing at the dream in front of him, he squatted down, grabbed a handful of fine white sand, and held it, letting the sand slowly slip between his fingers.

That night, Lisa and Paul dragged their exhausted bodies back to their shelter with nothing accomplished.

They walked through the noisy and cluttered yard and living room where, as usual, a group of young homeless hippies had gathered.

They were hiding here with nowhere else to go, taking comfort from each other.

They drank alcohol, smoked marijuana, played guitar, and made love.

Someone stopped Paul and handed over a thick mail, saying it had just been delivered by a local Black man.

When Paul opened the mail, he stood still, shocked, not believing his own eyes. There lay a stack of hundred-dollar bills and a postcard of Love Beach in Nassau.

There was no signature on the postcard. Just: *For Paul and Lisa's Farm.*

A23

"The old boat I ordered has arrived. StarCraft Chieftain. I've repainted her grey-blue and painted a new name on her." Charlie spoke to Bill through his ear implant.

"What's her name?" Bill asked.

"*Reflection*. Reflection of time and space. Reflection of our existence. Reflection of matter."

"Ha, what a perfect name!"

"Of course, it's also simple reflection, a contemplation. Anything you think of."

"Oh, I think I heard the rippling sound of the water."

"That's right. I'm already on the dock in the backyard. Everything has been loaded. I'm untying the rope. Will be out shortly. It was sunrise a few minutes ago. The overnight shower has stopped and only a few lingering clouds in the sky. The ocean should be quiet. I'm starting the engine right now. Talk to you later. It's too much noise."

"No problem. Talk later."

Charlie steered the boat slowly out of the peaceful bay that had just woken up from a deep sleep. The Caribbean Sea laid wide open in front of him.

The morning breeze brushed his face with the salty taste of the ocean. It was moist, warm yet cool, embracing Charlie, encouraging him for the journey ahead.

Charlie sped up. The engine began to rattle joyfully and freely. The wind blew against the overhead cover and the calm water was plowed into streaks of snow-white waves driven around by the boat.

He soon found himself in the waters off Love Beach. No one else was around. He was the sole insignificant existence sailing in the vast ocean under the humongous firmament.

The sun that had risen above the horizon a few minutes before, now turned into a golden flower, rapidly blooming like magic. Its reflections in the ocean were like the illuminated paths to heaven, sprinkled with bright golden crystals, extending to him from the unreachable sky.

All he had to do was to step forward and follow it, and peace would engulf him in its embrace. He would be happy and complete.

Suddenly, an emotion rose within him that he couldn't put into words.

He slowed down, made a circle, and then came to a complete stop to face the sun. He remained there, enchanted, watching the sunrise, letting the boat adrift in the gentle waves.

The golden blossom was now growing thin, dissolving in the rapidly brightening sky, losing its silhouette. In the blink of an eye, it was broad daylight.

Time was passing unaccounted for. Charlie checked on his wrist-watch.

"Bill, you still there?"

"Yep. Just had breakfast. Liz is cleaning the dishes. Let me get back to the office. Is everything okay?"

"Yes. I think I've found the spot for the quantum trajectory multiplexer."

"Near Love Beach?"

"About two miles off Love Beach. Outside the diving area and shipwrecks. The floor here is quite steep. There are many coral reefs, but it would be extremely hard to get to the bottom. I think this makes the most sense."

"What do you want me to do?"

"Stay on the line. The magnetic field of the ocean floor will be the ultimate test. We'll know in a few minutes whether it works or not."

"Sounds good. Good luck!"

Charlie stopped talking. He gazed down at the gently surging blue water; a bluish mirror waving with the swells.

The reflections of the clouds and the sparkles from the sun were floating on the surface, merging in and fading out mystically.

He leaned over the boat, trying to get a view of the deep bottom underwater but failed to see through the heavy waters. He imagined the bottom covered with fine white sand and short weeds with clusters of colorful coral reefs adorning the floor in all beautiful shapes.

He carefully took out the conch shell with the quantum trajectory multiplexer.

His eyes lingered on the ghost carbon Begonia flower for a second and he pressed his lips in a quick kiss on the conch shell.

As the boat rose and fell with the tides, Charlie stood with the conch shell, holding it over the edge of the boat. His arms still hanging over the water, finally, he let go.

The conch shell disappeared instantaneously on leaving his hands.

He could visualize it breaking through the surface of the ocean and slowly sinking into the water.

Cutting through the waving seagrass and shoals of colorful parrotfish, butterflyfish, and angelfish, it glided and landed on the reef. It tumbled once gently and came to a complete standstill.

It would no longer move anymore.

He could foresee it quietly staying there *forever*.

Days and nights would continue to fall and rise, and time would continue to flow. Nature would slowly claim the shell as its own. It would gradually be surrounded and eventually buried by the slowly expanding corals, grasping onto the conch for support.

It would eventually become a part of the reef.

No one would ever know where it came from.

No one would know *his story*.

It suddenly became extremely quiet.

He could almost hear his breathing and the sound of the sunlight splashing on the ocean.

He was gripped by fear, the fear of total failure.

"*Bill...*" He finally forced himself to call out softly.

He listened, holding his breath.

"*I'm here, Charlie.*"

Bill's voice came like a happy melody.

"Yes, I can hear you. Crystal clear." Charlie replied with a relaxed smile.

"How is the magnetic field?"

"Oh, don't know yet. Will test right now."

Charlie went down into the cabin and pulled out several instruments from a wooden compartment. A small magnetic sphere was attached to a tripod and a screen hung below it. Once out on the dock, Charlie set about assembling them quickly.

The delicate magnetic sphere was levitating and spinning, tracking the dynamics of the surrounding magnetic field.

The received signals were constantly processed in real time into a three-dimensional virtual image on the screen.

Charlie waited for a few minutes for the device to capture the waves. It showed an image of the magnetic field of the ocean near Nassau Island, a heat map that he knew very well.

The boat was being gently rocked by the waves as the ocean breeze flapped through.

Charlie locked his eyes on the screen.

"Bill, I got the sphere map."

"How is it?"

"Weird, don't see anything unusual."

"What? How could it be? The powerful solar storm is already brewing, affecting the Earth's magnetic field."

"I know. Wait a sec. Maybe I need to do one more thing."

Charlie slowly turned up a knob to bring up the sensitivity of the magnetic field detector above the normal range.

It hardly made any sense.

He had never done it before.

But right at the moment, the image on the screen completely changed.

It was no longer a calm image, but rather the Atlantic with roaring waves.

It transformed into a monster that had just been born, slowly rising and falling in deep breaths.

It almost turned scary.

At the same time, the instrument began to scream, bellowing in two high-pitched noises.

"Charlie, what happened? *Are you ok?!*" Bill shouted out anxiously.

"I *see* it, Bill.

I see a whirlpool of *space wormholes*.

It's amazing.

They are clearly still brewing, still small bubbles, but gradually growing and getting bigger.

They're like a swarm of newly born baby worms, worms of time and space.

I can't describe it in words, Bill!

Bill, it's all over.

Something *new* is about to begin."

A24

Charlie was woken up by a loud ringing beside him. He sat up to find his alarm clock striking five in the morning.

The darkness slowly dissipated before his eyes; his consciousness slowly emerging like an island from the sleepy ocean. A few minutes later, he turned on the light.

The blinding white light burst out, highlighting the calendar by the bed.

November 7.

Sleep still drowsed Nassau Island in the touch of dawn.

A thick fog from the Caribbean Sea loomed over the entire island.

Charlie slowly drove in the morning mist and stopped at the breakfast café that he had become familiar with. It was a hole in the wall, but at the moment it was lit up with a coveted warm light in the misty fog.

He pushed open the door. There was only a middle-aged Italian-American man standing behind the counter.

"Good morning, Charlie. You are so early today. We just opened." The man greeted him warmly.

"Good morning, Marco. Have to get going early today. You're the only one that would open at this hour." Charlie smiled.

"Certainly. The early bird gets the worm, or maybe, a hamburger?" Marco asked, his humor intact even in the early morning.

"Yes, please."

Marco placed the order at the cash register and disappeared into the kitchen. After a while, he popped up again and handed Charlie a hamburger and fries in a brown paper bag.

Charlie thanked him and was about to leave but stopped in his way. Marco was looking at him in somewhat a thoughtful manner.

Charlie paused.

"Charlie, have a nice day." Marco said.

"Thanks. You too." Charlie replied.

It was quiet at Love Beach. Not even the early risers had arrived to enjoy their morning stroll and the sunrise.

The Caribbean Sea was calm in the distance. The metallic grey-blue ocean was plated with the brilliant orange color of the sunrise. In the distant waters, a small yacht was vaguely visible.

Between the sky and ocean, seagulls flew by occasionally.

On the yacht, Charlie checked his time before returning his attention to the screen again.

It was still showing a puzzling wave pattern, completely different from the calm ocean around him.

Charlie locked his eyes on the blank swirls in the waves. Initially just barely visible, the tiny bubbles kept surging more and more violently now, secretly merging, trying to grow.

Not far away, a dolphin suddenly jumped out of the water and then dived back into the ocean.

"Charlie, a solar flare just happened. Omg, I can't believe it! I've never seen such a powerful explosion." It was Bill's voice.

"When will the released particle storm reach the Earth?" Charlie asked.

"*8 minutes*. You have 8 minutes."

"Okay. Got it."

"Bye, Charlie. *Good luck!*"

"Thanks, Bill. *Bye!*"

Eight minutes later, what Charlie had been waiting for, what he had planned so desperately and intricately, finally arrived.

The whirlpools on the screen all of a sudden began to merge with each other at an accelerated speed. It grew bigger and bigger in no time and was about to fill up the entire screen.

The original wave disappeared, silenced by a negative matter. It retreated to the corner and became a new blank.

The swollen whirlpool was surging, with an eager rhythm, as if it was living, breathing heavily.

It continued to grow at a horrifying speed, like the embryo of a bizarre extraterrestrial creature that had accidentally been awakened.

Then, everything on the screen was gone—*dead blank*.

Charlie could almost see those electromagnetic bubbles rushing out of the screen and spreading like a bright light throughout the deep ocean.

He quickly turned off the instruments, took them apart, and dumped the pieces into the water.

Without wasting a single moment, he dived in.

Charlie didn't swim away immediately. He turned to the bottom of the yacht, unscrewed a pre-set valve, and slowly stroked away.

He paused and had one final look at the yacht bathed in the fresh, bright morning light. It became tilted and slowly started to sink with water flooding in from one end.

Nothing left in this world that could hold him back.

He took a deep breath and plunged into the vast ocean, like a fish running for freedom.

Part Two Happiness
B1

CHARLIE DIVED INTO the ocean, stroking in his leisure, feeling the warm morning water graze his skin.

He didn't carry a scuba tank. He only had his goggles, snorkeling gear, and swim fins on his feet.

He drifted down like a falling leaf, deeper and darker, in search of the enlightening bubble.

The surface of the ocean moved farther and farther away as Charlie swam deeper, leaving only an obscured mass of light, reaching him from the just-blooming sun. It was like a distant, gigantic skylight that one could look up at from the bottom of a dark pavilion.

He could no longer hear the sound of the tide or the wind.

They were replaced by the sounds of various marine creatures amplified in the silence, snapping, crunching, squeaking, or thumping.

There were sharp whistles, crackling cracks, and dull thumps, or even melodious singing with syllables.

Lots of colorful fish passed by him, fish of various sizes swimming to their destined chores.

He saw the hazy silhouette of the deep ocean beneath him.

He paused to observe the almost fairytale-like beauty of the fish, living so leisurely and happily in the secret world of the ocean.

Thoughts of the mysterious red snapper now came to his mind.

The red snapper did not appear this time. But at the very moment, his skin felt a little itchy.

The water became more viscous and stopped flowing as if it had turned into gelatinous honey.

The fish around him stopped swimming, frozen up, like insects being trapped in the sap of a pine tree.

They were dissolving again. The shapes of the fish became blurred, like a frozen body of ice that was melting and dissipating under an unknown energy.

Charlie's own body was wrapped in the thick gelatinous honey, and he was no longer able to move.

He felt as if hiding in the distance, he himself was witnessing his own limbs become soft and transparent, losing their shape and dissolving away along with the colorful fish.

Once again, he experienced the separation of his body and his consciousness.

But unlike last time he was no longer frightened and panicking, not being able to understand the phenomenon around him. Instead, he was calm and felt nothing but pure, fulfilled joy.

He was shrinking again. The fish, the vague outlines of the top and bottom of the ocean, the translucent patch of light, all at once retreated far and far out of reach, like a telescope that was quickly refocusing.

He could see them no more.

He had shrunk into an extremely tiny existence, tinier than a microorganism, subject to vision only under a microscope.

At this moment, the bubble appeared.

Charlie's Bubble.

The bubble was glittering, like a dream, as if blown in the sunray's reflection by a street artist.

It kept stretching into the shape of a soft worm under the ingenuity of his skillful breathing.

As it detached from his device, the bubble assumed a spherical shape, freed from the shackles of the earth's gravity, and floated up.

His surroundings suddenly became barren and hollow, like an extraterrestrial vacuum.

The bubble seemed to be floating out of the ocean, out of the sky, engulfing the stars, glimmering and shining like a glittering ball.

It drifted into the gap between time and space.

Charlie couldn't hear anything anymore.

He was still shrinking, infusing into the play of the chaotic light and shadow.

His limbs, internal organs, face and feet were all left with a mess of molecules.

It was time that he ceased to exist.

Various vivid images now began appearing on the surface of the bubble, like movie clips playing from human memory. One clip flew into another, continuously and randomly, overlapping and repeating again and again.

His eyes were glued to the images. They were only occasionally familiar to him.

For one moment he saw the protest parade of the Chinese people outside the Forbidden City in Beijing.

Beijing in 1989.

Charlie's heart skipped a beat and almost jumped up to his throat.

He leaned forward towards the bubble.

Charlie's head and feet had now entered the bubble.

Now he could see the girl.

She was wearing a half-length haze blue dress and a creamy white shirt with her hair tied into a ponytail.

She had just come out of the courtyard and was walking towards the narrow alley lined with locust trees.

He knew that in a few minutes, she would meet him in the alley.

He wanted to lean in, submerging himself into the bubble, but suddenly a violent turbulence wrenched him away from his bubble, throwing him away from his dream. A whale had unexpectedly shown up, not far from Charlie in the Caribbean Sea. Swinging its huge body, it surfaced and plunged back into the water, creating a violet whirl.

Charlie hung on, swimming steadily towards the bubble. It was still there, pulling onto Charlie, merging with him. The surface of the bubble touched his skin. It was sticky and a bit soft.

But the bubble suddenly trembled as the water was agitated into deep waves.

Instantaneously the image lost control and started to swing on the surface of the bubble.

Charlie tried to follow the scene with the girl, but the images became more and more blurry, spinning in an unfathomable mass of mess.

She was about to disappear from his eyes forever in this life. There would be no chance of interception between her fate and his.

His heart ached, gripped by the claws of despair.

Without any hesitation, he leaped towards her image as it blended into a blurred fuzz.

B2

When Charlie regained consciousness, he was not in Beijing.

A busy commercial street lined with restaurants and shops made up his surroundings. The sky portrayed a clear day in the warm summer season.

He heard the familiar English around him, although the soft southern accent was missing.

A tourist bus painted in orange and green colors passed by, carrying a sign that said *San Diego City Tour*.

As his surroundings slowly came into focus, a single thought raided his mind.

He had to find Yinyi.

As he turned around looking for her, he noticed the reflection in the glass window of the cigar shop next to him.

The reflected image of the man looked *somewhat similar* to him. The man was handsome and charming, but *aged*. The hair was a little thin near the temple and the face might have grown wider over the years, suggesting the mutations of time.

The body was that of *a forty or fifty-year old*.

The man was staring at him.

As the realization set in, Charlie stared in shock and disbelief.

He waved to the man. The man waved back.

Charlie was horrified and stopped waving. The man stopped immediately too.

Charlie stood there and finally admitted sadly that the older man was *himself*.

He scanned around and walked anxiously up and down the street, looking for clues to find the time he had reached.

Finally, he found a blue newsstand on the street.

On the cover of the local newspaper, he read, *October 1999.*

Charlie was walking aimlessly down the street. The turbulence had thrown him way ahead in the future, eating up his youth and leading him far away from the woman of his dreams.

He found that he was no longer catching the eyes of the women passing by like a worldly wonder. Instead, they hurried by in their proud strides, completely unaware of his presence.

He was like a transparent shadow floating in the river of people, wandering in this strange year and unfamiliar land.

He felt even lonelier than the last time he was in Beijing in 1989.

But *what about her?*

Where is she?

He carefully recalled her image on the bubble now. It had appeared and disappeared in the chaos. He remembered the moment that he had jumped into the bubble: Yinyi was walking toward a light-yellow two-story apartment building with a small swimming pool behind an iron fence. Cars were pulling into a crowded parking lot in front of a grocery store on a busy street. A brief picture zoomed in, giving a view of the front of the store building- *99 Ranch Market.*

Those were all the clues he had to find her.

B3

Charlie was standing in the room next to hers in the apartment building.

His room was as small as hers, crammed with a bed and a chest of drawers. She walked past his door, catching a vague glimpse of him out of the corner of her eyes. It was the first time she had noticed him.

She had never seen him before. It was as if he'd suddenly dropped in from the air.

He was tall and straight, silent in the shadows, waiting for her to know him, to see him, to feel what he felt.

She kept going straight, not turning her head to him. But she could almost feel his gaze. She shivered a little, an unexplained desire rising within herself.

She had just settled in San Diego and rented a cheap furnished apartment on a short-term lease. It was a two-story, U-shaped complex building surrounding a small swimming pool, standing next to a busy commercial street.

The swimming pool was the highlight of the apartment, although no one was ever in the water. If there was one, he or she would be exposed to the curious gazes behind the windows of all the rooms.

She couldn't want that kind of attention.

Both their rooms were on the first floor. Anyone could walk right by the windows at any moment.

Her blinds were always kept shut, even in the daytime.

He met her for the first time next to the mailbox. It was there that they started speaking to each other.

His eyes fell on her young and attractive face; her eyes as clear as crystalline water.

The face that had never been blurred in his memory.

She had shoulder-length straight hair and was wearing a simple charcoal-colored shirt with a pair of matching casual pants that unintentionally outlined her curvy body with a tiny waist.

Somehow, he got the feeling that the country was still foreign to her.

That day, he slowly walked up to her door with a bit of hesitation.

She opened the door to greet him but was seemingly reserved, even on guard. Neither this place nor the people here were familiar to her yet.

He realized with sadness that *she had no memory of him. In her eyes, he was just a strange middle-aged American man.*

"Hi. If you don't feel comfortable, I can stand here and talk.

I've just moved in beside you. I'm not a bad guy.

I am Charlie."

"I'm Yinyi, I just got here too.

I don't know anyone. How about you?" She asked with curiosity.

"Me either." He replied.

He struggled to speak; all loss and despair forgotten.

All the difficulties and dangers he had pulled through did not matter anymore. At this moment in front of her, he felt more helpless than ever.

But he couldn't back down now. He wouldn't.

He glanced into her room and spotted two large suitcases piled on the floor, filling the narrow space between the twin bed and the window. The room was neat and tidy, just like he had seen in Beijing.

"Your room looks bigger than mine." He smiled.

"Really?" She also smiled.

"Do you want to go out for lunch with me?" He asked.

"I already had lunch."

"How about dinner? You have to have dinner, don't you?" He locked his eyes on her, insisting, encouraging.

She agreed to go out to dinner with him and got into his car. Charlie could still feel the reservedness emanating from Yinyi, but he was content just to be with her.

He moved away the laptop he was using for navigation from the passenger seat and in that instant, she caught a glimpse of a winding route marked on the computer leading to Louisiana.

They drove away to a Chinese restaurant near the apartment called *Panda Green*. In the dimmed lighting of the restaurant, they shared about their lives, getting to know each other a bit more. She told him that she was alone and that she had just finished her Ph.D. and was in San Diego for a postdoctoral job with a local university. For the moment, she was waiting for her work visa.

He confessed that he was also by himself and that he was the only child of his family. Both his parents had passed away and it had been only a week that he had landed a job in San Diego as a robot specialist.

While searching and looking for Yinyi in this unknown land, Charlie realized that he was a *nobody*. Here, he had no influence or reference. Looking for a way to settle down, he brought his passion into his workforce. Being a genius in mathematics and physics, he had enough skill to convince people around him to bag a permanent job as a robot specialist in a few months.

She expressed her amazement at his interests and innocently asked him about his past.

He frowned and with a lack of enthusiasm only briefly mentioned that he had had one formal girlfriend. That the relationship had lasted for five years; that the girl was mean, and they were always fighting.

Yinyi became quiet.

"I am a lone wolf." He described himself.

B4

A few days later Charlie took Yinyi out to hike a mountain.

It was a warm, sunny day. As they left the concrete paradise of the city and drove further away, the rolling green hills came into view, welcoming them in the embrace of greenery.

Charlie drove with one hand on the steering wheel.

Enya's song was playing, *"If I can be with you"*.

Charlie peeked a glance at Yinyi, sitting beside him. Her face, radiant in the womb of nature, her silky hair caressing her beautiful face, her eyes glowing in the reflecting sunlight. She was slightly bobbing her head to the rhythm of the passionate voice playing on the radio.

"Beautiful music." She said happily.

"I knew you would like it." He smiled.

As they began climbing the rocky pathway of the mountain, he took her by the hand, carefully guiding and guarding her, making slow turns and cautious advances up a section of rugged stone and sand paths.

The awkward silence was no longer there. A peaceful, comforting silence had spread between them which was occasionally broken by their conversations while walking.

He asked about her age. She let him guess. He said he could not tell the age of an Asian girl.

She laughed and said that she was in her early thirties.

On being asked the same question, he struggled for a moment and replied forty-eight.

Halfway down the trail they stopped to rest. The sun was pouring down on them. While Yinyi sat down on a rock beside the pathway, he stood tall and straight, shadowing her from the burning sun rays. His solid body was so close to hers that she could almost touch him without reaching out.

All of a sudden, an overwhelming desire to touch him washed down on Yinyi.

She breathed in the scent of his body, which was mixed with the sunlight and the fresh scent of the plants wafting in the breeze.

Warmth and desire flooded her body and mind.

The warmth thickened and exploded.

She began to melt.

They finally made it to the top of the mountain. Standing on the highest cliff, the world opened up to them, rewarding them with a 360-degree open view and a glimpse of the lower range of the surrounding mountains.

A queue had formed in front of them—couples and groups of friends were trying to take pictures in the best position for the view. On their turn, Charlie took a picture of Yinyi using a digital camera he had recently bought.

Likely due to the rush, the picture did not come out very clearly. Instead, it had the quality of something that had been blurred by the passage of time, just like their first meeting.

In the photo, she smiled beautifully though with a bit of shyness, her face blushing with the strain of exercise. Her long hair was blown up by the wind and she stood, bathed in the sunshine of the early winter afternoon.

His presence was only revealed by the long shadow cast on the ground, stretching out to her, reaching for her.

Christmas was coming and Charlie was getting to know Yinyi more and more. He continued to date her.

They visited the racetrack for the Christmas light show and drove around at night to check out the entire city, glowing in the joy of togetherness.

They would simply go grocery shopping together or just randomly go out for late-night rides. The night was dark, and the lights from the houses on the street flashed by. It was the lights of countless strangers, lights of a foreign land.

The abstract warmth of the festival felt exceptionally thin and distant. She watched the fleeting strings of bright lights from the car and was overwhelmed with loneliness.

She turned to look at Charlie, steering the wheel with one hand and his other hand holding hers tightly. In this foreign and still unfamiliar land, this man showed up in her life from nowhere, trying his best to give her all the joy, all the comfort she needed. A swelling warmth filled her heart, extinguishing the darkness of loneliness.

One night, as they stopped in front of the apartment building in the dark, he took her hand without a word, and led the way straight up to his own door. Their breaths filled the dark silence of the corridor as he took out the key, opened the door, and led her in. A switch clicked and soft dim light poured in.

Her eyes immediately fell on the queen-sized bed that almost occupied the entire room, leaving almost no space for hanging out.

He remained silent, still holding onto her hand. They took off their shoes and slowly laid down together, facing each other.

His face was right against hers, their breaths mingling together. He reached out and scooped her into his arms.

Their noses touched and she took a closer look at his face. It felt as if she had not been able to see it clearly until this very moment.

The straight and tall nose with neat and dense eyebrows framed a pair of exquisite eyes which were now locked upon her as if she was his whole world.

An unfamiliar and erotic temptation crept under her skin.

"*Charlie.*" She called his name softly, almost in a whisper, in a loving breath.

B5

" *Charlie.*" She called his name softly as if trying to confirm that he was real. That it was not her imagination manipulated by her lonely mind.

It was as if the moment the syllables of his name left her tongue, she accepted him and owned him; claimed him for herself.

The unknown about him was no longer an irrelevant blank for her, but a paradise where she was about to enter and explore her happiness.

She yearned for it.

Her voice touched him gently and shattered on him as if she was exploring him not only with her eyes, hands, and skin but also with her voice.

It broke into countless tiny pieces of desire and scattered in the dark night and the abyss she was longing for.

The room was immersed in a soft yellow light that had been dimmed down. Their bodies were vaguely visible to each other, more by touch than by vision.

There was no shame following the desire; only the wish to set it ablaze, set it free within each other.

Her body was overwhelmed by passion, passion that burned into her very core.

She could do nothing but yield to it.

She let him gently take off her clothes.

Her body was revealed like a beautiful piece of porcelain that was being offered to him as a tribute by her desire.

She laid completely naked, under his gaze in the dark, giving herself wholly to him.

She couldn't see much of his face.

She could see almost nothing.

No one uttered a single word. Both of them seemed to be completely drowned in the dark river of tranquil silence.

Without seeing each other, they were merging into one.

Strangers to each other, far away from each other, and yet so close.

He got up, pulled out a small bottle of lotion from a drawer, and spread some out on his palms.

She could feel his hands—strong and lustful, touching her body, and rubbing it patiently.

Slowly and meticulously, inching slowly towards her desire.

He was guiding her, lingering and taking plenty of time, coaxing, teasing her on the journey of bringing her to happiness.

Her inexperienced self was at his mercy, treasuring the touch of his warm hands.

Then he stopped.

He leaned over and kissed her.

She remembered when she was a child, her father had taken her to a lake in a pine forest, not far from home, and taught her to swim.

She had followed her father step by step into the lake.

The water was cool and getting deeper and deeper. It was gently rippling in the lazy evening sun under the shadows of the thin clouds.

The boundless lake was gradually sloping, filling up her entire view and was about to drown the sky above her head.

Her body began to sway and float like seaweed, losing its center of gravity and balance.

Nothing sounded in her ears except the sound of the rippling water, gathering and rising, floating her body with each wave.

She was swept away by curiosity and joy.

The joy of floating and letting it go in the boundless free water.

This time, she was again floating and submerging in the desire that suddenly rose in her like a tsunami and overwhelmed the sky above.

It was so powerful that it was almost destructive.

The sky was tilting again and disappearing over her head.

She was floating like a seaweed, a soft and long seaweed, a thirsty and eager seaweed.

Seaweed that kept growing in secret and flourishing into a forest.

Seaweed that was broken and reconnected in the entanglement with his body in the dark.

Everything floated up with her, even the most seemingly meaningless things levitated around her.

The bowls and plates in the kitchen, the wardrobe, the walls, the lights of buildings, the cars, and the shops on the street outside.

They all floated up with her and became weightless in the winter chill of southern California. They all floated toward the scattered stars, burning in the night sky.

It was pure indulgence in eroticism and pleasure.

And she, while dying, was being reborn.

The next day she got up early as usual. Following her routine, she went about her way to the research laboratory.

But her consciousness was still afloat when she was walking on the campus of the university. For some reason, the campus and herself felt like two irrelevant realities.

Around an obscure corner of a school building, she noticed a row of Clivia in full bloom of orange-yellow flowers.

She paused briefly in front of them.

They looked identical to the Clivia that her mother used to keep in a pot when she was a kid.

Years later, she would always remember the Clivia on the campus, and how she had felt herself drifting off the world of reality when she laid her eyes on it that day, and the feeling of being extremely light and virtual, as if she didn't belong to this world anymore.

It was a feeling of being suspended without being able to land—drifting away without boundaries.

It was a feeling of being evaporated by desire.

A feeling of being taken far away to a totally unfamiliar place.

A feeling of being filled and possessed by him who remained a stranger to her.

All these feelings, all in one, etched into her memory, becoming a part of her consciousness and her body.

B6

In the days that followed, he continued to spend time with her.

He would go grocery shopping with her and watch her cook with pots and pans in the cramped space of the tiny kitchen.

She would call him when the meal was ready, and they would sit down at the small round table that barely fit.

His body would struggle to find enough room and they would inch closer to each other, eating together, sitting face to face.

He would say nothing about his food preference and appeared to be perfectly happy with whatever Chinese food she prepared.

He loved the feeling of wrapping his arms around her, holding her tight to his chest.

You are a chemist. Tell me what kind of chemistry is making me so happy. He would bury his face in her hair and whisper.

Christmas finally arrived. Before meeting Yinyi, Charlie had booked a snowboard trip at Lake Tahoe and had to leave for Christmas.

He put his arms around her, saying that he hoped to hijack her to go with him.

She remained silent.

She stayed back home, left alone for Christmas, with only a bouquet he had bought her.

Remember, *I love you*, he had said before leaving.

There was no table or countertop in the room, so the vase was placed on top of the stacked suitcases by the window. The scent of the flowers wafted faintly with her memory of him in her humble studio next to the busy street.

The curtains were still kept closed.

She missed him, but she realized that she couldn't piece together the details of his face.

He was just a shapeless abstract being projected by her own emotions, like a shadow drifting in and out of her aching sensations.

Far and near, like a dense fog, he became a blurry memory.

Charlie returned in a couple of days and the moment he returned, he held Yinyi in his arms and pressed his face to hers.

His handsome face expressed nothing but his affection for her. It was the temptation she couldn't resist.

She suddenly had an illusion that someone else was hiding in the body that was hugging her, a mysterious and radiant man who was beyond her reach.

She looked up and gazed into Charlie's hazel eyes and saw the man hidden deep within. She stood, bewildered by his dazzling brilliance.

In such bewilderment, she believed that they had met and fallen in love in their previous lives.

She relayed to him that she was planning to move out. She had only been staying temporarily at the apartment on a short-term lease, and now she would move for a cheaper unfurnished option.

He looked into her eyes and said, "I don't want you to move away while I stay here. I don't want you to move to another place while I keep living in another.

I want to be with you Yinyi."

B7

Yinyi moved in with Charlie.

In this foreign land with no relatives, Charlie was the only one she had.

He took her in and gave her a home.

He held her tightly in his arms and murmured that before meeting her, he had thought he would be a lone wolf for the rest of his life.

He paid most of the down payment for their house. Yinyi was only able to make a small contribution but insisted that she and he must be equal, that she would draw a boundary, and not use the space she could not afford.

He watched her tiptoe, carefully bypassing the living room space and heading straight for the kitchen.

He frowned at her at first, then laughed and picked her up in his arms.

"You have no idea how happy you make me." He placed her gently on his big bed, leaned down, wrapped his arms around her, and whispered in her ear.

On their first Valentine's Day, Yinyi was working in the laboratory as usual when she received an unexpected call from the front desk. She had a delivery.

She ran downstairs and stood surprised. A large bouquet of beautiful flowers in a tall red vase with a heart-shaped pendant was placed on the countertop.

As she walked towards it, the woman at the front desk smiled at Yinyi and said that it was from a famous local flower shop.

Yinyi picked up the card kept on the flowers and read.

It was from Charlie.

Yinyi shared the laboratory with a group of international young researchers—Ben, an American young man who had graduated from medical school; Dawn, an American girl married to an Indian man; Chen Qing, a Chinese girl with big eyes and fair skin; and a couple who had followed the boss here from Cambridge, England to manage the laboratory.

The bouquet in her arms drew all the eyes to her. With shyness blooming on her face, Yinyi quickly fled out of the laboratory upstairs as if she was fleeing from bullets.

That evening, Charlie and Yinyi went out for an Italian dinner.

"The bouquet caused a sensation in the lab. All eyes turned to me. My fellow scientists gossiped all day. They said the bouquet must be quite expensive, especially delivered on Valentine's Day. It was a bit too much attention though."

"I want everyone to know that you are mine so no other man would dare to hit on you," he said with a sly smile.

It all felt like a dream that suddenly came true, except that the dream was a little illusory. Sometimes it felt real, and sometimes as if nothing existed.

After dinner when they got home, he gently pulled her into his arms and let both fall on the bed.

She ran her fingers in his light brown hair—soft and smooth, like cat fur.

He leaned his head into her chest, the furry softness coiling against her.

Her heart overflowed with tenderness. It was as if between her and him, she was in charge of this family.

But the moment he got up and his touch left her body, he seemed to be changing back to the man that she was still unfamiliar with.

A man foreign to her.

She got up from his bed and left for her own bedroom. Her room was pretty much the same as was in her small studio, with minimal furniture. The two large suitcases she had brought with her were again stacked in the corner of the room.

At first, he had looked at the simple setup of her room, puzzled by her reluctance to accept his offer.

"You seem ready to slip away anytime." He frowned. "Promise me you won't."

At this moment, her mind was occupied with his shadow, and she was still confused. She didn't know much anything about him.

She heard his door gently closing behind her. The noise was low and almost negligible, but to her ears, they sounded exceptionally clear and deafening. The moment the sound hit her ears, everything around her froze.

Her heart fell apart as if smashed by a blunt hammer.

It was the door to the Garden of Eden that had been slammed shut behind her. Along with it, the sun set, and the darkness rose.

In those few short minutes, she was bewildered for no reason.

It was as if he was a dimly lit train that had pulled onto the platform as she stood alone and waited.

As it stopped in front of her, the doors opened automatically, and she stepped in without questioning.

Only then did she realize that the insides were barely visible to her.

She wanted to see clearly what she had got herself into, but she was already on board, with no option of looking back, heading only to the future of unknowns.

Such conflicting moments always turmoiled within her, how she felt about him and how much she knew him.

After work, she would cook. They would chat over dinner and enjoy each other's company.

He always stuck close to her when she was cooking. She moved around in the kitchen but was able to see him busy on the computer in his bedroom or fixing something or doing fun crafts next to her. She felt at peace when his bedroom door was open.

He also spent considerable time on sophisticated equipment in the garage. She had no clue what they were, but according to him, they were related to his robot design projects.

Whenever he was working, his eyes would spark with an extreme focus as if it was the single most important thing in the world, and his hands would deliver nothing but rare perfection, intelligence, and refinement.

At those moments, he made her heart flutter.

She would call him when dinner was ready and they would sit together, eating and talking.

They had the ultimate happiness in the simplest form.

They followed each other like a shadow. Together they went shopping, to see a movie, and to the beach in a sunny bay.

He would place a folding chair on the beach for her, let her sit and read, while he put on his skates, made a charming turn with his body, and skated away.

They also invited her colleagues over for a party. Their usually quiet house was, for the first time, crowded with people that night.

Everyone was drinking, eating, and engaging in cheerful conversations. Ben brought his wife, the Chief Commercial Officer for a small company. Ben was born into a family of doctors. He was supposed to be on his path to a lucrative medical profession, but he preferred scientific research and would rather spend time in the unprofitable academia. It was a group of young intellectuals that shared their pure passion for science and the future, although their conversations bounced in all directions, and often erupted in laughter. Charlie noticed the glow on Yinyi's face when she was surrounded by her colleagues. They were her equals and she connected with them effortlessly. It reminded him of his time with Bill. It dawned on him that they were all fundamentally the same kind of people, talented, passionate, and with a genuine attitude toward everything in life and nature. And his soul and his body were drawn to Yinyi at the same time.

Late into the night the party ended with the kitchen left in a mess of cups and dishes. Charlie held Yinyi in his arms and told her how everyone liked her and had wanted to talk to her. He said it brought him back to the good old days when he was at home with his friends.

He confessed to her while holding her in his arms that she was everything he needed to be happy.

But the moments when his bedroom door would inadvertently close behind her would fill her mind with doubts.

She turned back and stared at the closed door, overwhelmed with the strange feeling that she was being kept thousands of miles away.

Those happy moments of love and intimacy suddenly lost their weight and significance at such moments.

The man behind the door was another man in another world.

The route from San Diego to Louisiana that he had marked on his computer when they first met, sparked in front of her eyes.

It must be connected to his past and his secrets.

Such a connection was only occasionally and inadvertently hinted at by him.

"Hometown strawberries are so sweet and juicy, best in the world." He commented with great nostalgia when he was chatting with her in the kitchen.

"Oh, I mean home in Louisiana." He clarified.

"But that's a thing of the past." He said sadly again.

It was at these moments that she would catch a rare glimpse of the hazy light in his memory.

"Are all your relatives in Louisiana?" She couldn't help asking.

Charlie didn't respond right away and instead kept eating his romaine lettuce and grape tomato salad.

She noticed the light dimming in his eyes. Not pushing him further, she waited for him silently.

Finally, he stopped eating.

"I am left with only a cousin three generations apart. And we have no contact with each other." He said with very little enthusiasm.

"How can that be possible?" She frowned slightly, thinking about the big Chinese families with scores of relatives.

"Everyone has a family. How can you have *no* family?" She was utterly puzzled.

"So that I can find myself a nice new family." He glanced at her warmly and quickly replied with a spark of happiness and wit in his eyes.

She heard the desire implied in his words, the desire to belong to each other, the desire that she also shared.

In the beginning it was nothing but lust. On their first night together, she had turned her back at him, facing the window behind the curtains and the dark night outside, struggling between her desire and her reserved nature.

She had let him undress her, the man who was a stranger to her.

She had asked him in a low voice, "Will you *marry* me?"

"Do you *love* me?" He had immediately asked her back.

She had no answer for him then. She was simply instinctively attracted to him, like a wild aimless lioness.

She did not respond.

But things were different now.

Before she said that she loved him, she had already been committed to him.

She didn't know the difference between the two anymore.

"When a Chinese loves someone, he will put his heart into it and *do* everything to make you *feel* loved. He doesn't talk the talk." She had said to him.

"That's cool." He replied.

But he only vaguely and occasionally hinted at his willingness to get married.

Except once, when he dreamed of Hawaii while snuggling in bed with her, he told her that he hoped to get married in Hawaii; that he had longed for a Hawaiian wedding.

But since then, he remained quiet about it.

It was as if he had casually dropped a spark, but now the spark was only secretly kept alive by her, quietly illuminating her bewildered life in her hazy subconscious.

B8

"B ill…"

"I am here, Charlie. Everything ok?"

"Everything's fine. Just that, I suddenly felt a bit nostalgic."

"I am here Charlie. You can talk to me."

"My body is old, but my mind is still stuck in 1978. You don't know how weird this is. It is almost like my looks are my clothes. They don't fit me, but I could never take them off. I am *trapped*."

"It will take time to adjust." Bill said reassuringly.

"Especially when she looks at me with so much love and tells me she likes the color of my eyes in the sun. I always forget that my body is no longer the same."

"I am making myself a fool, *am I*?"

"Charlie. She loves you the way you are."

"I know. That is why I'm so afraid. Afraid I'd let her down. I am afraid that I will be too old for her."

"Charlie. This is unlike you. You never cared much about women. On the contrary, you were always afraid that you wouldn't be able to get rid of them. You've given up everything for this Chinese girl, and you aren't sure that's enough?!"

"I *love* her." Charlie said in a low voice.

Charlie sat alone under an umbrella in the backyard. The shadow of the leaves of a luxuriant Ficus tree was caught on the umbrella, swaying in the gentle breeze. The scent of rosemary blew in the air.

Behind the backyard was a green valley stretching far away into the distance.

It was there that he talked to Bill via the ear implant.

He felt he could almost see Bill, across the spheres of time and space.

Charlie still played with various instruments out of habit. They were always his toys, no matter what age. His outlandish ideas of extensive experiments still existed, but he had no intention to pursue them. He was quite content with his present simple life.

It was a life for any ordinary man, making a living and supporting his family. He was there to take care of the nest he shared with Yinyi. They were there for each other hanging through the thick and thin.

This was new to him, but he could slowly feel himself embodying this new manner of life.

Yinyi soon landed a job with a local biotech company, an opportunity that she had longed for.

That night, Charlie took Yinyi out to dinner to celebrate. After the meal, Charlie held Yinyi's hand and walked out of the noisy restaurant.

It was a new moon. The warmth in his body resisted the slight chill that had begun to rise in the night.

He held her tightly by his side with his arm, as if to press her into his own body.

They walked up to the car. Like a gentleman, he went straight to the passenger side and opened the door to let her in.

Charlie had never been so content with his life. How happy he was that his dream had come true!

As he looked into Yinyi's eyes, his world lit up in a series of fireworks. But every once in a while, he realized that he had neither the past nor the future.

The flow of time had already been completely disrupted. It was like a small worm torn into many pieces, wriggling in a mess, in utter disorientation.

He had only *the present*. It was the lonely present, the present that was attached to nothing.

It was the present that was so blessed with happiness that it felt like an illusion.

It was the bubble that he had given up everything else for, a bubble that was floating alone in the empty interstellar space.

It was the bubble blown out by a street performer surrounded by children in a park.

It could burst any moment amid happiness and joy.

Once out of the happy bubble he and Yinyi were in, he could see the complete truth clearly; the emotions and sentiments driving at his heart.

Charlie learned not long ago that his Zemmuray estate had changed hands and become a local historical site.

And Bill... the Bill in 1979 who was chatting with him at this moment, would die in an accident while traveling in the ocean in 1999. Charlie found it in the obituary published in one of the local newspapers.

The newspapers would be digitized and lost in the vast and complicated computer network of information.

A network of cold and mechanical circuit pulses.

In 2000, Charlie bumped into that familiar name that unexpectedly appeared on the internet like a piece of small rock that he had accidentally kicked on a casual walking path.

He read on in shock and wept.

Life was like a fleeting moment. At this moment he held back his tears, looking out to the vast and empty valley.

But Bill was right there in his ear, listening to him anytime Charlie wished.

He could almost feel Bill's breath.

He had never thought before whether foreseeing the future was a blessing or a curse.

"Bill, you never asked me what America would be like in 2000. Aren't you curious? Don't you want to take the opportunity to change your life?"

"Why change? I am happy. Here and now, everything is just right." Bill replied.

B9

"*You.*

Watch me for a minute.
Watch the clouds next.
I feel that you are far away when you're watching me.
But close when you're watching the clouds."

Yinyi was watching Charlie dazing in the backyard, thinking of Gu Cheng's poem.

A swirling conflict bothered Yinyi as she gazed at her love beside her.

She was traditional and loyal by nature. She had stayed with Charlie and settled into a routine life with him. She was following the unspoken exclusivity rules, as if he was already her destiny.

But at the same time, she was completely unsure of their love for each other.

It came from nowhere and was rather loaded with a multitude of unknowns. It was like a fawn that miraculously showed up out of thin air in the woods.

It jumped around casually in and out of her view. It was unquestionably real and clear. But, right at that moment, she turned around, and it was nowhere.

She was tortured by such splitting doubts, unsure of what to think of their relationship.

Yinyi tried to dig herself out of her emotional predicament by denying her own dependence on him.

You are strong if you desire nothing, preaches the commandments of Buddhism.

She had tried going to the gym to play badminton or going out to a seminar with other boys or girls. It was easy to keep herself occupied as she was an attractive girl.

One night, she came home a bit late.

As she opened the door and got into the house, Charlie sat there smiling at her, like he didn't mind her spending time with other boys any more than she did.

It would make more sense to her that he would be a little upset so she could feel his desire to *own* her. But he was never an ordinary man.

Yinyi was relieved that he did not react to her struggle for her own independence from him. As it turned out, she found that the more she spent time away from Charlie, the more she longed for him. She painfully acknowledged that she could not deny her own feelings for him and was already disabled in her efforts for her equal position in their relationship. Consequently, she was no match for him.

She could not eradicate her desire for him after all, even if he was still both close and unfamiliar.

The desire in her body continued to surge and almost overwhelm her.

She would be able to do nothing but yield to whatever fate was waiting for her.

Yinyi stood at the kitchen counter, dwelling on her uncertainties when Charlie entered the house from the backyard, looking exclusively attractive. He walked in and stopped in front of her.

The sunlight coming in from the window hit his face, turning his bright hazel eyes into translucent emerald.

He hugged her from behind. Lowering his head, he pressed his face on the back of her neck.

Love and desire rushed through her blood, although her reserved nature barred her lips from confessing the words swirling in her mind.

She suddenly heard him sobbing quietly and her own struggles were immediately forgotten.

She turned around out of concern and looked up into his misty eyes.

"I just found out I lost my best friend, my only childhood friend," he said.

Her face coiled in concern. She hugged him tenderly, trying to comfort him.

"In this world, you are the *only* one I have.

Let's get married Yinyi," he said unexpectedly.

B10

Instead of Hawaii, Charlie and Yinyi went straight to Las Vegas to get married in the Little White Chapel.

"It's easiest and fastest in Vegas," Charlie told Yinyi.

Their wedding was improvised and causal, without any prior preparation. They were like two young kids eager to do something in haste while for everyone else it would be a serious once-in-a-lifetime event that deserved extensive planning.

Yinyi informed her parents over the phone. She sent them pictures of Charlie and received their blessings remotely.

The wedding couldn't be any simpler. In addition to the female pastor presiding over the ceremony, there was also the Chen Qing couple, two local friends of Charlie and their wives, and an organ player sitting in the back.

Yinyi was dressed in a bright red sleeveless Chinese cheongsam, holding a bouquet in one hand. She had found the cheongsam at a local Asian clothing store and had the tailor alter it to fit her figure. According to Chinese tradition, red symbolizes happiness, she told Charlie.

She secretly prayed that she and Charlie would *be happy forever.*

With the priestess' blessing, Charlie and Yinyi exchanged their rings. Charlie's ring was a little tight, so the priestess applied some skin care lotion to help Charlie put it on.

The atmosphere couldn't get any more casual. They were following through the pre-scripted ceremonial process that was more procedural rather than romantic.

It wasn't until the ceremony was over that the priestess led them to gather beside the organ and sing in joy. Charlie held Yinyi by his side and listened attentively. Dressed as a bride, holding Charlie's hand, Yinyi's heart was overfilled with happiness.

That night, they were invited to watch a spectacular indoor dance performance as a wedding gift by their friends. When they returned to the hotel, the stars were scarce in the dark night sky outside the window, but the city below was still with millions of lights sparkling and shimmering.

Charlie held Yinyi in his arms, his eyes fixed on her face.

"You are beautiful." He whispered, overwhelmed with emotions.

Their life was now bound together, *forever*.

Charlie put his heart and soul into his life with Yinyi. He was busy at home with the renovation and yard improvement. He went out with her to music, movies, and workout. They traveled the world together and tasted the local cuisines.

It was an ordinary life for everyone, but he loved every minute of it. It was the most beautiful way he could have lived.

He was getting used to her being by his side. It didn't matter if she was doing something or nothing. As long as she was there, he was content, complete, and happy.

After getting married, Yinyi moved into Charlie's bedroom. This move might seem trivial for the other American couples, but to them, it was of great significance.

Giving up their individual space, their privacy, and opening up to each other was the most initial step in becoming one together.

It had been almost unimaginable for Charlie in his past.

On the bed was Charlie's favorite dark brown comforter. It was elegantly designed, fluffy and warm. It smelled exclusively of Charlie.

The entire bedroom was hidden behind the total blackout curtains and kept in dimmed light.

It was Charlie's own safe haven.

He could never sleep with any of the other women he was with, including Jennifer.

In his mind when a person was sleeping, he was completely unreserved, fully exposed, vulnerable, and original. So, he had to be alone, had to preserve that vulnerability.

Now he had Yinyi lying next to him in the dark night, falling asleep with him.

They faced each other, kissed goodnight, turned off the lights and fell asleep. She leaned into his arms, holding his hand, only letting go when her consciousness became hazy.

He always slept on the right side, and she, on the left side. In deep sleep, she sometimes turned over, occasionally kicked a leg over, and unconsciously grabbed the comforter tight, as if she was particularly afraid of the cold.

He heard her shallow breathing, her occasional turning as if turmoiled in sleep. He saw her vague silhouette in the night.

He could reach out and touch her. He could feel the warmth of her body, take comfort from the fact that she was by his side.

It brought him peace and security.

He grew used to it unconsciously and didn't think much about it until Yinyi left for an academic conference two months later. He was home alone, guarding the empty bed. Out of habit he reached out, but his palms only touched the cold sheets. He again felt the ancient loneliness rising within him.

Only then did he realize that he was no longer the solitary and complete self he used to be.

She was already quietly becoming a part of himself, part of the medium and context in which he existed.

He was no longer free.

He was no longer the one single individual. Everything was in pairs now. He bought two of each, identical computers and cell phones. He bought hiking shoes or suitcases of the same brand for both.

For any trip they planned, he would prepare everything for her along with himself, be it toiletries, rechargeable batteries, or luggage tags.

Everything was in sets of two, side by side, shoes by the treadmill, charging cables for the computer, or towels in the bathroom.

The sign of their companionship was everywhere in the house.

There was a photo he took in Yellowstone Park. It was a clump of scorched yellow weeds standing alone in dry and cracked land.

He had shown it to Yinyi and told her, "*This used to be me. Now, I have you.*"

B11

That May, Charlie and Yinyi drove to Mammoth Mountain for a skiing trip. Before the trip, he insisted on taking Yinyi to the REI store and bought all the outfits for her from head to toe: soft, warm, and breathable fleece, windbreaker jacket, an insulation layer for the upper and lower body, and Smart Wool socks.

He was familiar with name brands and was never willing to compromise on the quality of a product for a lower price.

During the conversation, he mentioned that his wardrobe used to be a gold mine.

But when Yinyi took the opportunity to inquire about his past, he quit talking.

The Mammoth Ski Resort was covered by the last snow of the season. Charlie got dressed and left the hotel, heading to the ski slope.

Standing outside the crowd, Yinyi watched him take the ski-lift with his skis in his arms and fly like a bird down the rolling snow mountain.

She stood there, searching for his figure among the numerous moving dark dots on the snowy slope, following him intently.

He moved his body with ease and charm. He was free and strong.

She was overwhelmed by her love for this man.

Finally, the tall and handsome man finished skiing, took off the skis from his boots, and walked straight back to her.

"You've been standing here all this while? Isn't it cold? Let's go inside. You can have hot chocolate and warm up by the fireplace," he suggested tenderly.

Back at the hotel, the staff at the front desk greeted them and casually mentioned a newly opened bus route to Yosemite. Charlie immediately booked two tickets.

"I have long been longing for Yosemite, but never had the chance to make the trip. I can't miss this opportunity." he said to her in excitement.

Yosemite in May was considered off-season with very few tourists.

Charlie and Yinyi roamed around in the valley. He took her to the famous Half Dome Cliff and Bridal Veil Fall. They visited the Ansel Adams Museum where he commented with admiration that Ansel was a great photographer.

Later they rode on a tram for two hours, listening to the tour guide.

Sitting by his side, Yinyi gazed at the profile of Charlie's face, at his tall and straight nose, and his beautiful eyes with long eyelashes. She slightly leaned her head on his shoulder, absorbing the aura of his love.

Behind him, pine forests and magnificent cliffs passed by.

One word came to her mind as her eyes lingered on him. *Grace.* Yes, there was absolute natural grace about him.

It was natural nobility.

It was not only good or sexy looks, but also reservation and appropriateness. It was neither humility nor arrogance. It was fundamentally humane and warm but yielded to no external force.

It was decency and authenticity, all merged into one.

It was like a diamond, crystal clear, authentic, natural, and pure. It would shine even in the most forgotten darkest corner of the world and brighten the entire universe.

She was still baffled by his presence in her life and by his past, but she no longer struggled with it.

All she knew was that she *loved* him.

She was hopelessly in love with him.

B12

Soon it was their first time celebrating the Chinese Mid-Autumn Festival together.

Yinyi picked up her favorite Cantonese-style moon cakes and fruits from a local Chinese market.

That night the two of them nestled in the wicker chairs in the backyard to watch the moon, following the Chinese tradition.

The orange-hued full moon was hanging low in the evening sky, like a gigantic streetlamp, not far from them.

Charlie looked cautiously at the moon cakes on the plate. He picked up a piece, savoring it in his mouth, and paused.

"Does it taste ok?" Yinyi asked curiously.

"It's ok."

Yinyi understood immediately that he didn't like it.

They had acquired different tastes before they met and couldn't be any more apart from each other when it came to food.

If having the same preference for food was a criterion for a couple to be allowed together, they would not have even the slightest chance.

Charlie picked up a bottle containing a dark creamy drink, poured it into a small glass filled with ice cubes, and handed it to Yinyi.

"Try it, you'll like it."

"What is it?" Yinyi looked at the glass, hesitating. She did not drink at all.

"Baileys Irish liqueur," Charlie answered.

Yinyi took a cautious sip. It was a sweet and smooth milky drink with a hint of chocolate. It felt warm and soothing to the throat.

"Tastes good. I like it." She spoke.

But soon, the alcohol started to work. Her face started to burn, and her body was melting.

Charlie was watching her. "I wasn't sure if you would like it, so I poured only a little bit for you. You want more?"

"No more. I might be drunk already." Yinyi replied, feeling the heat gathering on her cheeks.

Charlie smiled. "How can you be drunk? It wasn't even enough to cover the bottom of the glass."

"I'm just drunk. I get drunk as soon as I drink. That's what happened in the past. If I drink any more, my body will collapse."

"If you collapse, I will take care of you." Charlie said with a sly grin.

But he stopped talking, a subtle spark emerging in his eyes. It flickered and merged with the moonlight that enveloped them.

He put down the wine glass and pushed it away together with the moon cakes and fruits.

He brought Yinyi to him, put his face on the back of her neck, and began to kiss her.

It was warm, moist, a little slow and a little tickling. It was like the first note from the plucked strings, or the initial sporadic raindrops preceding the storm. It was a sudden rising tide of desire.

Yinyi greeted him, like a quiet and hungry plant greeting the rain, leaning back against him. His strong arms wrapped around her.

The full moon was shining more brightly like a flower blooming in the night sky.

Yinyi bent her body toward him, overwhelmed by the rising darkness, the full moon and Charlie's desire at the same time.

She couldn't tell whether she was disintegrating into alcohol or lust.

It was as if a whole river was raging and boiling from inside her body, trying to push out toward the full moon and into Charlie's body.

It was the joy of approaching heaven.

She leaned back and reached out, aimlessly stroking his hair.

"Let's go in." Charlie whispered warmly in her ear and carried her into the house.

B13

October. 2018. New Orleans.

Forty years since Charlie's Bubble experiment.

Walking on the streets of the French Quarter of New Orleans, Charlie slowly drifted forward, walking with a bit of difficulty, yet pulled in by the memories of the place. Old age had greeted him in a pleasant way. His handsome face, now wrinkled, still showed the lines of his youth. His eyes still bore that same spark, though his body had weakened now.

The street was in the shadow of the past, with a dilapidated and nostalgic atmosphere, as if it was stuck there, forever, in time.

He recognized several old restaurants such as the Galatoires or the Commander's Palace, which symbolized the city's preserved prosperity.

He saw more walls deteriorating into ruins and heard the melancholic jazz that never stopped haunting this corner of the world.

He saw people who tossed their frustration behind their mind, drinking and cheering, mingling with the soul of the city.

The souls of those who had once died of yellow fever were also alive in the sarcophagi of the mausoleum, listening in the evening twilight.

It was like an old videotape, which kept playing backwards, and the city had forgotten to move it forward.

Charlie had an illusion that he was going to bump into the younger version of himself at any time, who was walking over with Jennifer in his arms, unrestrained and lost in pleasure.

He soon found himself standing in front of Wilson's stereo store. He hesitated for a moment, but then mustering up his courage, he pushed open the door.

An unfamiliar middle-aged man came up to greet him.

"Is Mr. Wilson still here?" Charlie enquired softly.

"You mean the old Mr. Wilson? He retired and passed on the shop to me. My name is Wilson too. Is there anything I can do for you? We have remodeled the sound room. Would you like to come in?"

"Oh no. I'm just passing by."

So many things were different now. He realized that he no longer had any more ties with this city.

Charlie suddenly felt relieved from the nostalgic complex that had haunted him over the years.

He felt terribly homesick, wishing to get back to his dear Yinyi.

When Charlie landed in San Diego that night, it was almost ten o'clock at night.

At home, Yinyi was trying to stay awake for his return.

"I am taking a shared ride. Not sure where we are but for sure still running around in some other neighborhood. Go to bed honey. I will see you tomorrow." He texted her.

"I'll wait for you," she insisted.

More than an hour later Charlie finally arrived home. As she opened the door to greet him, he leaned forward and kissed her.

His lips felt moist and cool.

"I rushed back. I was afraid you might be getting used to not having me around." He said.

"It's not that easy."

"That's good."

"We've been together for almost *twenty years*."

"*Not long enough*." He murmured.

In the past twenty years, they had gradually grown into each other and merged into one like two intertwined trees.

He had retired as a senior executive from a local company whereas she had risen to the mid-management level.

But as the years passed, neither seemed to have grown old. Instead, they grew into two children who had little concern about the rest of the world and were madly in love with each other, happily spending their lives together.

As usual, he was sitting downstairs watching TV when she walked over to him in a white bathrobe after her shower. His eyes immediately moved over to follow her, like a sunflower trailing the sun.

"Squeaky clean." He announced for her, with the warmest smile on his face.

She smiled at him, meowing twice like a cat with a sweet voice. Her hands were spread out to her sides and swinging in a silly way, mimicking a baby bird flapping its short wings.

He was watching and smiling with sparks of joy in his eyes.

She flung herself into his arms like a little bird.

"You smell good," he said, sniffing her long, wet hair.

She pulled her hair back carefully, moving it out of his way. She then rested her head on his chest with her left arm wrapped around his neck.

Her soft, petite body curled up on him like a cat, nuzzling closer to his warmth.

His body, strong and warm, made a very comfortable bed for her.

She was resting on him like a baby that had no worries in this world.

At moments like this, she could forget everything and just fall asleep.

It wasn't lust. They were attracted to each other's bodies in such a special, tender, peaceful, and emotional way.

He had slowly become attached to her presence. It was comforting for him to just have her around him, simply there in his vicinity where he would take her into his arms or kiss her.

They were attached in every way that was possible for two human beings to merge into one. He loved her. His love was bursting out like a full moon, without any shadow or flaw.

He fell asleep on his recliner, while the show on the screen playing out silently. It was his favorite show about the universe. He was wearing headphones so Yinyi would not be disturbed.

As sleep slowly drowsed him, his head fell onto one side of his shoulders, burying his neck, with one hand half clasped and the other spread on the side arm of the chair. His laptop was left open, resting on his chest, rising and falling with his breath like a butterfly's gentle flap of wings.

He looked old in that position, like a body from which life had been drained out. But yet, he looked as fragile as a baby that had no guard against the dangers of the world. He had no retreat or reservation, completely submitting himself to her and her mercy.

She was not sure why she always saw the seven-year-old boy on his clearly mature face: slightly raised now with distinctive, handsome features, the light of happiness pouring out from his eyes, bright, dazzling, and pure, without a trace of impurity, haze, or shadow.

It was exactly the same. Nothing had changed. Even though he went from seven to seventy.

It was as if his aging skin was merely a meaningless disguise for his still innocent soul.

That was what she saw when he smiled at her, expecting her to nestle into his arms.

That was the look in his eyes that never failed to melt her heart.

She gently covered him with a thin blanket and went to bed first as usual.

Sometime later into the night she woke up. In the darkness, she could vaguely spot his figure approaching, his light, whispering footsteps.

He was as quiet as a mouse and was moving his body carefully, in an extremely slow motion.

He first quietly landed on the edge of the bed, then paused, sitting there motionless with his back facing her, like a sculpture of silent shadow. He then turned sideways, and started to slowly lean backward until his whole body was gently laid down on the bed, as if the bed was as fragile as an eggshell.

It took him almost two full minutes to complete the move that would otherwise be done in two seconds, so he wouldn't wake her up.

She remained quiet just like him in the dark, as if she wanted him to believe he did not disturb her at all, and he was, in every way possible, the most loving man a woman could have.

B14

Charlie could always feel the passage of time. It did not pass away silently, but with a sharp rustling sound, making its presence known as a quiet mouse in the dark that kept gnawing.

It had no mercy. With perseverance, day and night, it kept biting into his time with her, leaving it *shorter and shorter* with every passing day.

He was afraid of the end that was bound to come.

He was prepared to leave the world before her; not having to see Yinyi taken away from his life would be the last mercy that time would allow him.

That night she walked up to him while he was sitting downstairs. She lifted her head, touching her throat with one hand, and said, "I have a bump here."

He stared at her, spotting a bump bulging out from her throat.

His face suddenly became strange, as if the flowing water had suddenly frozen into a mound of ice. He didn't move; didn't know where to look. He seemed to be suddenly petrified and turned into a stone sculpture.

She continued to talk to him while moving closer to him. But she quickly noticed his change.

She looked more closely at him and saw that his eyes were filled with tears.

He remained motionless. His nose twitched, but he did not turn to look at her. It was as if his body was placed under a dangerous spell- if he moved even just a little bit, the tears in his eyes would overflow so much that they would flood the entire world.

She held back her tears.

She immediately went onto the internet on her phone and after quick research, she said that it might possibly be a thyroid nodule. She read to him calmly what she had pulled out, as if it had nothing to do with herself.

He appeared to be listening. But he didn't speak a word, his body remained as stiff as before.

She got up and left for upstairs.

Just as she was about to step on the stairs, suddenly, she heard him burst into a loud cry as if he was collapsing like a broken dam.

It was a cry of doomsday that she had never heard before, a cry of ultimate despair.

It was a cry of a broken family and a broken heart.

She stopped and wept with him.

Fortunately, on getting the tests done, it later turned out to be a false alarm. The bump on Yinyi's throat was not a tumor, and soon with time, it would dissolve on its own.

It was one of the episodes in life that would be quickly forgotten, except for Yinyi, it weighed on her how he was emotionally crushed by such a slight threat to her.

On a Saturday morning, she woke up early as usual.

She got up and went downstairs, settling down on the couch, ready to work on her laptop.

To her surprise, flames burst out in the fireplace at this moment.

She smiled.

She knew it was him who started the fire from the bedroom upstairs. All her life, she could not help but wonder, how this man so strangely came into her life and built his entire life around her, the center of his world.

She felt him everywhere, and every minute. He was the air she breathed in to live and the floor she stepped on to stand.

He would do everything for her, unasked, of his own accord. His entire life revolved around her. Even when her conditioner would run out, she would find it quietly replaced by him. Before she could ask for anything, he placed all her necessities, all her favorites piling in front of her. Charlie only lived for Yinyi. That night, she went downstairs and found him sitting on the chair without looking at her. She went up to him and snuggled in his lap, looking up straight into his eyes.

"I love you." He spoke.

B15

Early January 2019.

Rain poured down tremendously, the temperature dropping sharply to the 40s.

It rained three times a week. Hail mixed with the rain and bounced on the glass windows.

The sky was gloomy.

Against the south wall of the backyard, the two bougainvillea planted the previous year unexpectedly bloomed with some pink flowers, looking fully alive.

This was the first time in years. The previous bougainvillea had never survived more than a year.

Charlie's tall frame was eventually attacked by his arthritis which broke out often, causing immense pain in his back, neck, and hand. But these pains were invisible to the naked eye. He kept working around the house, creating an illusion that he was still a strong man for her, the man she could count on.

He was almost 70 years old, but he was not like any other ordinary old man at all.

He was helping her with everything, from weightlifting and moving bulking boxes, to taking the trash out every week.

He said that he wanted to take care of her when he was still able to.

At this moment, sitting in his chair, Charlie said it was going to rain again and he wasn't planning on working in the afternoon.

"Don't worry about work. Get some rest. You are not getting paid anyway." She commented jokingly, trying to comfort him.

But he thought for a few seconds.

"Honey points. I earn honey points." He blurted out, coyly.

Soon it was 2020, and their twentieth wedding anniversary amidst the Covid pandemic. The viral pandemic of coronavirus had overtaken the entire world, confining people to their houses, taking away millions of lives.

Charlie prepared a card and bought a necklace with a crystal heart pendant as a gift for her.

He was sitting at the small glass round table by the backyard when she leaned into his arms like a little girl.

He put his head against her, holding her tight, and whispered to her how much he loved her and how lucky he was.

At this moment, desire seemed to be awakening like a beast from its deep sleep.

His hands moved onto her body, caressing and exploring.

"I love you," he whispered to her. "*I love all of you.*"

It had rained heavily the day before, flooding many parts of the city.

He drove her through the water-logged streets to pick up food from a Greek restaurant. Out of concern over the raging virus, she insisted he stay in the car and wait for her.

The restaurant had a small front. Yinyi put on a face mask and gloves and walked in. A couple of boys were busy in and out of the kitchen and a few customers were waiting in line. Everyone was wearing a mask and carefully maintaining social distancing.

One boy behind the counter told Yinyi they had run out of rice, for the first time in all these years. On asking Charlie, he confirmed that he would not want it if there was no rice.

It was past seven o'clock in the evening. Yinyi baked up small Canadian potatoes, warmed up frozen pork ribs, and made corn and egg drop soup for their anniversary celebration.

He fell asleep on the chair, looking vulnerable and helpless. He looked aged, as if life was being folded up in his body.

She wondered what would happen if he left her like this. Would she be the only one in the world whose heart would be truly broken by the loss?

If so, would it be true that the significance of his life was exclusively for her alone, his only family?

In the end, everyone was insignificant and would be forgotten by the world, including her and him.

All the important tasks, the dead truck battery to be replaced, the water heater to be repaired, and the beef stew and potatoes that she had just learned to make, were they all serving the exclusive purpose of the private life and happiness *between him and her only*? Once they were both gone, those endless chores would instantaneously become meaningless.

It turned out that the significance of life was entirely personal. It was fleeting and meager. In this mere existence, he and she depended on each other, and were profoundly significant for each other.

It turned out that they lived only for each other. It had almost nothing to do with everything else in the world.

B16

Charlie and Yinyi drove up the west coast of California.

Nine hours of driving seemed extremely long. They kept changing from one section to the next, but the road seemed endless, going on and on. Charlie felt exhausted. His neck and legs became sore.

It seemed that the tall and handsome man who was driving across the vast land of California was an unrelated false appearance, the tireless appearance that had nothing to do with him.

The illusion of the strong man that Yinyi was used to.

His body underneath, however, had been unknowingly eroded by time and become hollow.

It's just that the hollowness wasn't evident to the eyes and the invisible pain was not fathomable.

She was sitting beside him, checking out enthusiastically the scenery along the way, while eating snacks from time to time.

They drove into San Jose.

The traffic in the urban area was unusually light. Due to the frequent rains, it was lush green with exuberant trees everywhere, in contrast to the drought often seen in southern California.

Yinyi caught a glimpse of his arm stretching back, his neck rolling over his shoulders. He was apparently trying to rub the stiffness out of his neck.

"You want me to drive?" She asked softly and cautiously, in an effort to avoid challenging his ability.

He said nothing.

She looked at him, concerned.

He reached out and patted her leg.

"I'm fine." He assured her.

The inn on Moss Beach was half an hour away. They were headed for the cloud-topped west coast in the evening hours.

Rain started to pour down when they made their way onto the coast in the dark and began a series of sharp turns.

There was constant oncoming traffic, throwing blinding lights on them. Charlie slowed down significantly out of precaution.

Finally, they saw the Seal Cove Inn, brightly lit from a distance.

The inn was quiet but well-lit at night. In the lobby, a fire was burning in a beautiful stone hearth. There laid a set of cozy white sofa and chairs and a Christmas tree decorated with holiday lights.

There was no front desk as commonly seen in regular hotels.

Charlie and Yinyi eventually noticed a desk with a pair of sofa chairs in the corner to their right. A clear acrylic shield was placed on the desk to block direct contact due to the ongoing COVID-19 pandemic.

Behind the desk, a casually dressed elderly woman was busy on a computer, with her back facing them.

She turned around and greeted them kindly.

The next day was cloudy and rainy. But when it was close to noon time, the rain clouds and fog unexpectedly cleared, letting in a bit of blue sky and white clouds.

Charlie and Yinyi were overjoyed and decided to go to the Martin Beach immediately.

It was from a sunset photograph that Charlie first learned about the beach. In the picture, a brilliant ray of sunlight was caught piercing through the cave of a huge black reef called the Shark's Tail, making a splash of golden sparks that were like the light from heaven.

It was an image that Charlie never forgot.

And as always, he heard the call from the wonderful nature and traveled all the way to be there.

Charlie and Yinyi pulled up at the intersection of Coast Highway 1 and a path leading to Martin Beach. Car entry to the path was however blocked with a sign marking private property.

He checked out the roadblock. He had heard that a wealthy man had bought this beach and started to ban the public and that the man was in the middle of a lawsuit.

"It's a shame for any individual to monopolize such natural beauty. Everyone should have equal access to nature, regardless of being rich or poor." Charlie shook his head and commented.

Carrying a heavy camera bag, Charlie walked ahead, passing through green fields and seaside houses.

On the sandy beach, a few hands away, Charlie spotted the Shark Tail Reef.

It looked like a gigantic black shark that was slowly sinking into the roaring ocean, with only its tail sticking out of the water at the moment.

He was astonished and quickened his pace.

Yinyi followed behind, making stops here and there. Contrary to Charlie's focus on nature's wonder, Yinyi was fascinated by everything along the way: houses under the tall cypress trees, blue paintings on a stone wall, and the leafy vines climbing over on the rocks on a white sandy beach.

When she stepped onto the beach, Charlie was standing right behind a split, looking down where the sandy beach was unexpectedly cut open.

The cut was clean as if done by a sharp blade. The opening was several feet wide with water flowing through.

Behind Charlie, some wild bushes were tangled in a mess.

She walked up to Charlie.

"The best angle for the camera is over there." Charlie pointed to a cave in front of the Shark Tail Reef on the other side of the cut. "Too bad the path is broken. We can't cross like this."

Charlie set up the tripod, positioned the camera towards Shark Tail, and started taking pictures.

Dark clouds thickened above. The tides roaring and rising. The wide beach was almost entirely deserted except for the two of them.

Moments like this were always his happiest time: he with his Nikon camera, fully immersed in nature.

Nothing else would come close to his mind, neither the human world, nor himself.

It was the return of his soul, his recovery, his reconciliation with time.

It was the significance as well as the pleasure of his being.

Over the years Charlie had traveled to numerous places for photography. Iceland, Easter Island in Chile, Patagonia in Argentina, Alps in Switzerland and France, Machu Picchu in Peru, and Angkor Wat, to name a few. Sometimes he traveled with Yinyi or friends, sometimes alone.

He was always seeking a great shot, an image he stripped and created from the visual mess perceived by the ordinary eyes, an image that pleased both the eye and soul and brought them to a new world.

It was a dream that never stopped growing within him. It was sometimes silent, sometimes loud, but was always there, unwilling to die, even when he had turned into an old man from an ignorant boy.

He seemed to have been under the spell of Mr. James throughout his entire life.

Mr. James had said there was nothing more fun than photography, creating your own world with images. In such creations, fleeting moments were frozen into eternity, outliving ourselves.

Yinyi wandered around, taking random cell phone shots for her documentary.

Her eyes were drawn to Charlie. Still tall and handsome, he had a sexy look to him when he was laser-focused on the camera.

He was still the man who took her breath away.

They returned to the Seal Cove Inn but went out again for a walk to take advantage of the fresh blue sky, a break from the rain and the cloudy gloom.

The hotel was located in Marine Cypress Reserve. The Pacific Ocean was only a few minutes away on the other side of the sky-reaching dark green cypress forest.

The cypress trees lined up row after row. Their branches stretched over and intertwined in the air, forming a gigantic canopy and a tunnel beneath. In the sun the dense shadows of the trees were cast on the damp ground, cold and wetness extending all the way.

It was like a mind-blowing scene in a movie.

Charlie again walked ahead and continued to be the favorite subject in Yinyi's paparazzi shots.

He was going in and out of Yinyi's field of vision, walking like a child, bewildered by the wonders of nature.

Out of the blue, Yinyi recalled a scene from a Chinese TV series that she had recently watched. In the scene, a young couple first leaned on each other, looking out to a lake. But in the next minute, the boy disappeared, leaving a void in the picture.

The girl only stood there alone.

Charlie and herself would not be there for each other forever and either one of them would leave a void in the other.

It would be unbearable loneliness. Yinyi felt her heart constricting at the very thought, forcing herself to keep these thoughts away.

But the ocean, the cliff, and even the cypress forest would always be there, hundreds of years, thousands of years from now. They were simply there witnessing an extremely transient moment that belonged to Charlie and herself, as well as the few tourists around who were also indulging in the happiness of life. But the moment would fleet by and be wiped out.

The thought was so in conflict with the wonderful time they were having and so disturbing that it terrified her.

Yinyi instinctively forced herself out of that thought.
She walked up to Charlie quickly and let him take her hand.

B 17

Charlie and Yinyi planned to spend two nights in a B&B in Crestline, a mountainous area near Lake Arrowhead in southern California.

The day before the departure, the hostess of the B&B sent a text message, saying that the local utility company had cut off the electricity as a precautionary measure for the strong wind, low humidity, and the escalating fire hazard. She mentioned that she had a generator and still had hot water and electricity, but the central heating was out. However, she had put a portable heater in the room, so they did not need to worry.

Charlie immediately lost interest and had second thoughts about the trip. Yinyi, however, was quiet. Charlie realized that she had been looking forward to the trip after busy working the whole year.

"We'd better go," he said. Charlie couldn't say no.

On the road, he first played Dido's songs. Ever since he found out that Yinyi had become Dido's fan, he had been playing her songs for driving. He even dug out Dido's concert videos and watched them on TV.

"You still like Dido, do you?" He asked.

"I like Sunlounger now," she replied.

"Great. My honey likes Sunlounger now."

He immediately switched to Sunlounger.

He kept driving. Yinyi suddenly noticed that his right leg seemed to be shaking.

She couldn't believe what she saw. She must be mistaken she thought.

She stared at his leg.

It was still shaking, involuntarily.

She immediately reached out and held his leg.

"*Are you shaking? What is happening?!*" She asked aloud, horrified.

"It's been like this for a while. Sometimes it just does it." He mumbled, not surprised at all. "So are my hands. I don't know what it is."

His words sank her into a pang of indescribable sadness.

She didn't want to ask anymore. She didn't want to get to the bottom of it.

She became afraid, afraid of the truth, afraid of him wondering about the truth, and afraid that neither he nor she could do anything about it.

When they approached the mountains, the wind suddenly became violent. The leaves on the top of the tall palm trees were flapping like flags. Sand and dust were flying off the ground, blowing up into the air, and raining down on the windshield of the car.

They had got into the lodgings. Crestline was covered with immense pine forests. Their room faced the west, with sweeping views overlooking the rolling hills and the city below and beyond.

Outside the glass sliding door was a wide wooden balcony. On the balcony stood a small table with a flowerpot and chairs, as well as an egg-shaped rocking chair and a double rocking chair.

Bird food on a board hung from the eaves. All kinds of birds flew around, resting and feeding on the eaves.

She was excited and immediately stepped out of the room to check out the rocking chairs.

He stood inside and looked out. He seemed to have something on his mind, she thought to herself.

For the first night, they stayed inside behind the closed curtains.

They finished their dinner at five o'clock and darkness descended outside.

Soon Charlie found out that there was no hot water.

After exchanging text messages with the hostess for the whole night, there was still no solution.

The generator was humming. Now and then the noise would become blunt, as if the generator was too exhausted to stay on. For those moments, the wall lights beside the bed would begin to flicker, and the TV screen would go out briefly and come back on.

They had nothing to do and went to bed early.

It was sunny the next day. They drove to Lake Arrowhead.

The lakeside was mostly a private zone except for one area that had been developed for tourism. Decked with a clock tower and beautiful European-style buildings, the area was packed with boutique shops and restaurants. It was here that tourists usually gathered.

Charlie parked the car and said, "I will follow you, honey. Go wherever you want."

As proposed by Yinyi, they went straight to a small restaurant by the lake for lunch. Wide glass windows facing the lake allowed a panoramic view of the lake and surrounding trees.

He sat down with her at a small table and started to take off his blue surgical mask, ready to eat.

Yinyi suddenly felt vulnerable and nervous, when she watched him removing his face mask with a few people behind him.

She was sensing a hanging danger, life-threatening viruses, invisible to the naked eye, floating in the air.

She was struggling with the impulse to walk out.

After lunch, they took a walk by the lake.

Charlie was following Yinyi, but he stopped to stare at a group of ducks and birds on the lakeshore.

It was quite an interesting scene. Green-headed ducks mixed with black and white birds, had gathered under the railing, waiting for people to throw down food.

Among them were a few white geese, swaying their plump bodies, quacking dissatisfiedly.

Charlie stared at the white geese and spaced out. He told Yinyi that the geese could be really fierce, and that he was attacked by a bossy goose when he was five or six years old.

She saw again in her mind the handsome little boy, the little boy frightened by an aggressive goose.

The defenseless little boy whose bright eyes always melted her heart.

The little boy who entrusted her with his life.

After Lake Arrowhead, they went to hike in a pine forest.

The lush pine trees possessed the quality of a sophisticated blend of ancient grace and resilient life. They stood straight and tall, seemingly stretching into the clouds above.

Charlie and Yinyi stopped immediately to take pictures of the beauty around them. Charlie took a few pictures of Yinyi standing in front of the ancient pine.

They soon found the inception of Will Abell Memoria Trail and began climbing up the mountain.

A few youngsters behind them quickly caught up, overtook them, and disappeared in front.

Charlie walked slowly and hesitantly on the winding path between the pine trees before he simply stopped. His eyes wandered into the distance.

Yinyi walked up to him.

"I'm tired. Let's take a break. I don't know from when, but I am starting to feel dizzy when I climb." He said, frowning down at his chest.

"Not sure if it's because of my diet change or something else." He added.

She knew that he had recently been on a calorie-restricted diet. She did not want to think beyond it. Rather, she was afraid to think more about it.

"Must be the change of your diet." She replied immediately, in an attempt to comfort him.

But as soon as she finished her sentence, she was overwhelmed by a deep secret sadness. She now knew that he buried all his worries quietly in his own heart.

He greeted her every morning with a smile and kept her ignorant of his pain.

Both he and she instinctively avoided the topic of pain. Nobody wanted to mention or face it.

They both opted for pleasure like a phototropic insect opting for light.

But the pain was always there, lurking in the dark. Moreover, with time passing by and with aging and deteriorating health, it grew deeper and heavier.

It turned out that life would always be *a lonely journey*, and even more so in the face of pain.

It was hard to survive a lonely journey, even more so for a close couple like them.

They returned to their B&B.

He walked with her down the wooden stairs to the hillside garden of the house to look out.

The blue sky was decorated with white clouds above, but the distant horizon was already tinged with muddy orange. The sun was soft, like a sunset.

He walked over to the bench at the edge of the slope and sat down.

The sunlight instantly melted him into its soft golden color. Behind him were two luxuriant old trees, towering tall over his figure. Both his body and the trees were leaning toward the vast but indistinct mountains and plains ahead.

At that moment, he seemed golden, brilliant, out of reach, like the first time she met him—the handsome man who burned an unspoken desire within her.

The man she fell in love with at first sight.

That night, he and she took turns taking hot baths.

He walked into the bathroom while she soaked in it.

Her body spread out in the bubbling water, revealing everything before his eyes.

His eyes seemed to discover something he had forgotten.

Something that had been quietly hiding under his nose.

Something that had been lost for a long time.

He knelt by the tub and caressed her.

His hands seemed to have awakened life in her, his and her life, a life of youth and lust.

He watched her body twist under his touch. Her beautiful full belly was rising and falling.

At that moment, they seemed to be returning to the old days, when both wanted to give each other nothing but pleasure and happiness.

She had a dream that night.

She was chatting with a female colleague and a female middle school classmate about going to her company together.

Suddenly she heard an explosion.

Fire flickered in the distant streets.

Pedestrians looked around helplessly.

Someone whispered in her ear that something might have happened to the buried explosive.

Suddenly a huge and strange image appeared in the sky. Lots of sparkling magnetic field lines, one stretching to the other. It was steaming, like being scalded in the air by a hot iron.

In the horror of the moment, she thought of nuclear fission.

She saw the pedestrians who were standing till then, dropping to the ground one by one, from far to near, like a row of knocked down dominoes.

She instantly realized that it was a nuclear catastrophe from which no one could escape.

Death was before her eyes.

She had only a few minutes left in this life.

She thought of him immediately, hoping to say goodbye to him and tell him that she loved him.

She picked up her cell phone and called him.

The call went through, but the voice she heard from the other end was strange, unfamiliar.

Her heart sank into the abyss.

"Where is he? Where is he?!" She cried out insanely.

At this moment, her whole world collapsed. It collapsed even before the destruction touched her.

B18

It was around ten o'clock and Charlie was watching the grand finale of Lilyhammer, a TV mini-series with his head resting on Yinyi's shoulder.

Unexpectedly he found Bruce Springsteen in the show. Charlie got excited and immediately dug up the videos of Bruce's old performances to share with Yinyi.

"You may have heard this song. Or this one!" He said to her.

But Yinyi's eyes had begun to droop. It was time for her to go to bed.

Charlie put on the headphones to continue to watch TV when she rose and went upstairs to bed.

She was already lying down when she got a call from him. He had never called her after going to bed in their twenty years together.

She heard him cough violently downstairs.

"I feel bad," he told her hastily on the phone.

She hurried downstairs. Charlie was not on the sofa.

She ran to the bathroom and found him on the floor, holding onto the toilet, vomiting violently and uncontrollably. She reached out to feel the temperature on his forehead. Her palm was covered with his cold sweat.

Dizziness, vomiting, excessive cold sweat.

"I'll take you to the hospital." She said, panic settling in.

"Call 911." His voice was weak.

The ambulance arrived in a few minutes with some strong young men wearing N95 masks and light-yellow protective gowns.

They checked Charlie out immediately and very soon had the stretcher ready to take him away.

Yinyi wanted to go with him but was told that due to the pandemic, the hospital was not allowing any visitors.

She rushed to find him his driver's license and medical insurance card.

Pale and weak, he spoke no word, silently being carried on a stretcher. His charcoal T-shirt was lifted, exposing his torso where a few probes were attached for medical monitoring.

She brought him his black down jacket, afraid that he might be cold.

She stood on the street and watched him being taken into the ambulance.

It was a very dark night. Everything was immersed in darkness, except for him on the stretcher, exposed by the bright light inside the ambulance.

He was completely passive, helpless, and weak, at the mercy of others. He showed no emotions, his face coiled in pain and stress.

She was standing in front of him.

Suddenly it hit her that this was the last she would see of him before they took him to the hospital. What happened after that, she would have no clue about it.

Suddenly she bent over with overwhelming sadness, as she subconsciously though reluctantly realized that there was a one in a million chance that this might be their last moment together.

The thought broke her down almost immediately. Streams of tears streaked down her face.

She leaned in and whispered to him that she loved him. She then touched his feet and said, "Honey, please hold on."

He, however, seemed to be no longer aware of her.

He was taken away. She slowly walked back to the house and closed the door.

She was left all alone.

She didn't know what to do. This was the moment she had been afraid of all her life.

She couldn't think or sit down. There was no recourse. She couldn't settle on doing anything.

She kept wanting to cry.

The sadness in her chest kept surging up and down, like a sudden gastroenteropathy, or vomit that was about to burst out. But the sadness was held back by anxiety for a while. She swallowed it down again and again.

It was simply stuck in the throat. It was stranded there, with nowhere to land and nowhere to vent. She was in a state of extreme confusion.

She took out her bag and placed in some face masks and gloves. She got dressed so she would be ready to go to the hospital to be with him as soon as required. It might happen at any moment.

When she had mechanically finished all her preparations, an hour and a half had passed, and the hour of midnight was long gone.

She took out the map that the paramedics had left for her and told herself that she must figure out how to get there.

After this was done, she collapsed on the couch downstairs, still holding onto her phone, expecting a call soon.

Another two hours passed, and it was already the early morning of the next day.

She realized there wouldn't be any calls. And she would not be able to go anywhere after all.

B19

Early next morning, Yinyi located Charlie's room at the hospital. Her call went through. He had been tested negative for COVID-19.

Over the phone Charlie informed Yinyi that the entire floor downstairs was filled with Covid patients. The doctor was still arranging various tests for him, trying to figure out what the problem was. Everything that had been tested thus far was fine, so there was no need to worry.

It all sounded like good news and cheered her up a little. He made it sound like he was just taking a break in a hotel. His voice was relaxed and delightful.

"I finally got a chance to look outside." Charlie said.

"The windows are so big. You can't imagine how beautiful the outside view is! I can see the valley stretching far away, the blue of the mountains, and the plains... so green.

By the way, I recognized Highway 78, and I finally figured out where I am. The ambulance went round and round for a while that night. I thought for sure I was taken to a hospital far away.

Yes, it is very nice. The hospital is new and modern; almost like a hotel. If it wasn't for being sick, I would have loved to stay here with such a beautiful view and see the world with you.

Sure, I'll take some pictures for you shortly"

At this moment, a sudden siren sounded with a code blue call from the corridor behind Charlie.

Charlie's voice stopped for a moment.

For almost half a minute, Yinyi could no longer hear him.

"Charlie, *is something wrong?!*" Yinyi shouted in panic.

"I didn't want to tell you dear, but I, I'm afraid the time is up for me." Charlie's voice suddenly turned gloomy.

Yinyi felt like she had just been hit by thunder. She collapsed into tears, breaking down on her knees.

"I wish I wasn't this sick useless old man. I wish I were your age, young and strong. I wish I could spend many more years with you and make you happy."

His throat was choking. Tears rolled down his eyes. He struggled to complete his words.

"Forgive me.

Life is too short.

Remember, I love you.

I will come back to you."

Part Three Forever
C1

NOVEMBER 1978. NASSAU.

The Love Beach on Nassau Island was shrouded in the gorgeous thick colors of sunrise.

A beat-up local fishing boat was sailing to the Caribbean. On board were two young Bahamian men, dark-complexioned and strongly built.

They noticed what seemed to be a small boat floating on the water in the distance.

"Did you see it? It looks like a yacht. Wow, one expensive yacht!" One of them exclaimed.

"That's weird. It just stays there, like a floating statue. Does not look like there's anyone on it."

"Maybe another bored rich man lying across the boat. He probably had nothing to do and came out here in the middle of the night to kill time. Doesn't he have anything important to do?" The second man who was manning the boat grumbled.

Out of curiosity, they started to sail toward the small yacht.

But right before they got close to it, an incredible thing happened.

A figure stood up on the yacht, then jumped into the water and disappeared quickly. The yacht swayed a little later and started to slowly sink.

Stunned, the two fishermen stopped their boat and watched.

In an instant, the man driving the boat accelerated sharply, approached the yacht, said something to the other guy, and jumped straight into the ocean.

When he reappeared on the surface of the sea, he was holding Charlie in his arms, deflated and passed out from lack of oxygen.

Charlie opened his eyes. Clear sharp white light hit his eyes and he squinted, trying to get a clearer vision.

He was lying on a single bed, with a needle inserted in his arm, getting an IV drip.

That arm was muscular, and the skin was firm and clean, free of the brown age spots.

He immediately stretched out his other arm and looked it over carefully.

Did time turn back? Did he regain his youth?

The thought hit Charlie like lightning. A surge of joy welled within him.

But as the realization settled in, a burst of sadness quickly followed.

He was lying in a very shabby ward with cheap yellow paint on the walls. A medical chart was taped to the wall in front of him.

He stared at the picture carefully. Its footnote said: *Hospital West.*
Nassau Island.
The Bahamas.

"Welcome back to 1978, Charlie. It's been five days and five nights. You finally woke up." Bill's voice sounded warm in Charlie's ear.

"Did you bring me back?"

"No. It was the local fishermen. Lucky you."

"No. It was *you*. I know it, Bill!"

"Ok. It was me. I can't just sit still and watch you die.

I can't do it.

I broke your bubble with a magnetic wave."

"You broke *my entire happy life*. A life of *twenty-one years*." Charlie moaned, closing his eyes, sinking his head into the hard hospital pillow.

"It was *three minutes*, Charlie.

Please forgive me. You and I will never have another chance of a solar storm in our lifetime. You will never see her again. It was an accidental contact between two different wormholes. Her time looped back to ours through your virtual bubble. But you do understand, I just barely got ahead of the God of Death.

Charlie, listen to me.

Go back to Zemmuray Garden. Everything you had is still there. Nothing has changed.

Forgive me. I have not executed any of the wills you had asked me to. You didn't travel to 1999, marry the Chinese girl, or turn seventy. You simply had a long vacation and a long dream on Nassau Island. Montgomery is still taking care of your garden, waiting for you to come home."

Charlie breathed a long sigh. He couldn't think of any words to answer.

Charlie's car pulled into the wrought-iron gate of the Zemmuray Gardens.

Mr. Montgomery was talking to a gardener on the lawn when he heard the noise and turned around.

"*Charlie!*" He blurted out in excitement and immediately limped toward Charlie.

Mr. Montgomery appeared to be thinner, with deeper wrinkles on his forehead. Adding to his old age were his unshaven face and gray hair.

Only his eyes were sparking with joy, like a flame of happiness that had somehow risen within him.

It felt like another life.

Charlie was completely confused about his identity at this time.

He was not sure which was real, and which was a dream—the 30-year-old him or the 70-year-old Charlie that had lived a perfectly happy life for almost twenty-one years with Yinyi.

Were both his dreams? Or were they real? They existed simultaneously, overlapping and connecting with each other, inseparable.

What was standing in front of Mr. Montgomery was obviously his 30-year-old young and strong body. His soul, however, was old and crushed by the agony that he and Yinyi had now been separated forever by time.

Every piece of memory was still there, intact and vivid. Her looking up to see his smiling face; her soft body leaning into his arms.

He seemed to have exhausted everything in his love for her. He had no other life left.

The man that was with Mr. Montgomery was only a living carcass of him.

It was simply an illusion, a fake substitute, a reprogrammed soul disguised as a mere husk of himself.

A walking zombie that was full of sorrow.

His eyes reflected both joy and sadness, drowning in the ultimate confusion, ultimate conflict.

Mr. Montgomery became aware of Charlie's strange behavior.

He stopped and looked at Charlie one day. The joy on his face gave in to bewilderment.

"Charlie, is everything okay?" He asked uneasily.

"Everything's fine. Nice to see you again." Charlie forced a smile and replied.

C2

Taking his routine shower, Charlie went down into the Game House.

Everything remained the same; just as he had left them. Various instruments, utensils on the marble table, books and journals on the shelves, all stood in their place.

When he saw the old rotary phone on the desktop, he couldn't help but smile. He picked it up, dialed it, and put it down again.

His eyes turned to the huge whiteboard on the wall.

His handwriting was still there.

November 7, 1978.

Charlie's Bubble.

Charlie's heart was racing. He walked over, picked up the scrub brush, and slowly, little by little, wiped off the handwriting; wiping off every chance of getting back to his Yinyi.

The phone rang out loud suddenly. Charlie was taken aback, but instinctively picked it up.

It was Jennifer's voice. It was both familiar and strange, drifting in from the past life that had long been buried by the dust of time.

She said she was getting married. The groom was the pilot Charlie had met when he last went to her house. The man loved her so much that he changed his job and moved back to New Orleans.

"I owe you an apology for what I did, Charlie. I just never felt so defeated when I realized you never loved me." Jennifer confessed bitterly.

"Jen, it's been over a long time ago. I don't even remember it anymore." As Charlie spoke, he realized that it was him in his 70s speaking.

"Oh, I mean, I'm happy for you. You met the right guy who makes you happy." He quickly adjusted his tune.

"I wanted to send you my wedding invitation. But will you come?" She asked.

"Definitely. Why not?" Charlie smiled.

Jennifer's wedding was held at a small Catholic church near New Orleans, witnessed by twenty formally dressed family members and friends.

To the sound of the wedding music, Jennifer walked into the church in a white wedding dress, holding her father's arm. She cast a glance at Charlie as she passed by him.

Charlie greeted her eyes with a blessing smile. He felt as if he was attending the wedding of a friend with whom he had long lost contact. His heart, however, could not connect to anything around him.

It was all over, first as a thing of the fresh past, then forever forgotten and erased, as if nothing had happened.

There was always a new life, new excitement, and new events to fill the momentary void left by any individual in this world.

Charlie was part of the picture of happiness. He was praying and blessing together with everyone else.

At this moment, he was warm and kind, wishing everyone in the world happiness.

The sunlight filtered in through the top stained-glass windows, flooding across Jennifer and her new husband like a river of colors.

Under the guidance of God and the pastor, they promised love for each other for life and beyond.

On their sides were the bridesmaids and best men who were as beautiful as angels.

But hidden in the countless color pixels of this picture of happiness was something so tiny that it was invisible to the passing eyes.

It was a huge hole in Charlie's heart, a gigantic void that was unrelated to the happiness around him.

C3

October 1999. San Diego.

The young Yinyi came out of the 99 Chinese supermarket and drove onto the road.

Her eyes were drawn to an apartment building on the street. It was a two-story, U-shaped apartment, surrounding a small swimming pool.

The sign in front of the rental office read: *For rent. Furnished. Vacancy.*

On the spur of the moment, Yinyi quickly parked her car on the roadside and went inside.

The apartment manager was short, gentle, and polite. He took out a ring of keys, opened the door of a studio on the first floor, and let Yinyi go in to have a look.

"This room is ready for moving in. Rent is good, only five hundred and fifty," said the property manager.

It was very small, with barely enough room for a twin bed, a side table, and a dresser. Further inside was a tiny kitchen and a bathroom.

Yinyi was standing in the room, looking at the swimming pool immediately outside the door, hesitating.

She seemed to be seeing something, or maybe nothing.

Little did she know, by the will of God, right here, two months later, Charlie would show up at that door, ask her out to dinner, and that would change the course of the rest of her life.

That is, if Charlie's bubble hadn't been aborted by Bill.

Now, the script of her fate had been revised.

She would *never* meet Charlie in this life.

She decided against the apartment and left.

Yinyi settled down in San Diego and started working in a research laboratory.

She was busy reading the electrophoresis film when Chen Qing came over with a private express mail for Yinyi.

Yinyi opened the package to find a thick photo album lying at the bottom of the package.

The photographer had traveled to many places, first quite a few locations in San Diego, the apartment building near 99 Ranch Market, a mountain, the site on which the laboratory building where Yinyi was working was built, except, that it was still a piece of undeveloped land.

Following San Diego, it was one American national park after another, Yellowstone, Bryce, Zion, and many more. Many European destinations followed, a few Asian and South American countries, including China, Peru, Argentina, and finally back to San Diego.

Those photos were obviously taken years ago. In Beijing, China, the streets were flooded with people riding bicycles. It was a familiar memory for her.

The sender had also enclosed a letter with the package. Yinyi opened it and began reading.

Hello Yinyi,

I am Bill from Florida. The photographer of the pictures I've sent you is Charlie, my best friend.

You might not believe this, but Charlie and you have met each other in your previous lives. He lived with you for twenty-one years and both of you were madly in love with each other. He was later forced back to his own time and since then, he has been trying to collect the memories from all these places that he had visited with you. Charlie spent ten years from 1980 to 1990 tracking and recording the footprints of his future life together with you.

Charlie had promised that he would come back to you when you two parted. He was waiting to meet you again in 1999 from his own time but he died unexpectedly during an outdoor trip.

This album is a message bottle left by Charlie for you to find in the winding and twisting river of time.

It now carries the bits and pieces of his memory and love for you. This is yours and I have been trusted to send them to you.

C4

Year 2045. San Diego.

The elderly Yinyi left her son's family.

It was August 19th, Charlie's birthday, according to Bill's notes.

While she read the letter, she didn't know why she had believed right away that she had, indeed, met Charlie. It was an ancient memory that she did not know about, that had been quietly locked up outside her consciousness, and had collected a thick layer of dust over time. Only bits of it had flashed occasionally in her dreams. But it had always been there, as an ultimate mystery to herself, until now, when Charlie finally came to her, or rather, *came back to her.*

In 1999, when she stood in the small apartment near 99 Ranch Market and looked out of the door, she had already seen Charlie.

He was tall and handsome. He smiled at her from the doorway and left.

At that moment, she already knew that for the rest of her life, she would miss him alone.

She came to Del Mar.

She first dined at Il Fornio, Charlie's favorite Italian restaurant, then leaving the bustling shopping mall, she drove to Torrey Pines State Beach.

She entered the park, parked the car on the hill, and slowly walked up the path on the cliff toward the Pacific Ocean.

Her body was no longer fit and her back always hurt. She unconsciously hunched a little.

It was around five o'clock in the afternoon. Young people passed by her on the path from time to time. No one paid much attention to a small, old, Chinese woman.

She and Charlie used to hike on this trail, she remembered now. In the summer, the air was always a mix of the heat from the sun and cool and salty breeze from the ocean.

It used to caress her skin, bringing her unspeakable joy.

She sat down on a wooden bench lining the trail and looked out at the ocean, surrounded by low vegetation, and the Torrey pine trees, which spread out their dense branches like the wings of a huge bird.

She kept sitting there, watching the sun go down first and the night rising and swallowing the ocean.

The entire park emptied, and the entrance was closed. She was left alone, sinking into the dark and cold night.

She remained motionless in the night wind, holding Charlie's photo album in her arms.

Slowly, she fell asleep, giving in to the clasp of the deep, cold night.

She felt her body shrinking, thinning out, almost glimmering from within. Slowly, pleasure filled her body and a smile tugged at her lips.

She did not wake up. She was with Charlie in their bubble.

And they were happy once again.

The End
(January 2023)

Author's Note

The story is for all those who are anchored to this world by someone they love. How we long for being with the one we love, forever, when our actual life is fleeting and the significance of ourselves might be fuzzy. Time travel is our way of aspiring to go beyond the limitations of the physical world and life, to find something emotionally eternal.

If you like the story, I would greatly appreciate that you leave a rating or review.

bekaflynn8@gmail.com

About the Author

Beka Flynn has two passions in her life: science (the mystery of nature) and literature (human emotional beings in the form of language). Beka Flynn is a PhD scientist, and a writer.